Cell
Block
Five

Cell Block Five

Fadhil al-Azzawi

Translated by William M. Hutchins

Arabia Books
London

First published in Great Britain in 2008 by
Arabia Books
70 Cadogan Place
London SW1X 9AH
www.arabiabooks.co.uk

This edition published by arrangement with
The American University in Cairo Press
113 Sharia Kasr el Aini, Cairo, Egypt
420 Fifth Avenue, New York, NY 10018
www.aucpress.com

First published in Arabic in 1972 as *al-Qal'a al-khamisa*
Copyright © 1972 by Fadhil al-Azzawi
The moral right of the author has been asserted
Protected by the Berne Convention

English translation copyright © 2008 by William M. Hutchins

Chapters 1 and 2 appeared in a slightly different form in
Banipal: Magazine of Modern Arabic Literature no. 28, Spring
2007.Chapter 4 appeared in a slightly different form online at
wordswithoutborders.org, May 2007 edition;
currently archived.

ISBN 978-1-906697-03-7
Printed in Great Britain by J. H. Haynes & Co. Ltd., Sparkford
1 2 3 4 5 6 7 8 9 10   14 13 12 11 10 09 08 07

Cover design: Arabia Books
Design: AUC Press

One

When I turned toward the policeman sitting beside me in the patrol wagon, he asked a bit sarcastically, "Are you one of them too?"

The policeman's face looked dark in the twilight of the spectacular evening that had been descending on the city for more than an hour. When I looked at him calmly, without hatred or affection, I saw that he was smiling in a way that seemed quite barbaric. He was smoking tranquilly, as if he wasn't a policeman and as if his left arm wasn't resting on his rifle. He sat near the wagon's door on a long horseshoe-shaped bench that circled the interior. I said nothing. I didn't feel like talking. I was overwhelmed by a painful sense that everything was ruined and that I was lost. The policeman tapped me on the shoulder and said, "Okay, you're scared. Never mind. But why did you incriminate yourself?" I was struck by a deep fraternal feeling for this policeman, who wouldn't hesitate to shoot me in the back if I tried to escape.

I said, "I'm not afraid. I was arrested by mistake three days ago and I will certainly be released soon."

One of the five other arrested men laughed scornfully and asked, "If they intend to release you, why are they sending you with us to a penitentiary where prisoners are kept for long periods?"

Two other policemen intervened. The first said, "That won't prevent him from being set free after a week."

The second one commented, "They released three of my prisoners yesterday. When I said goodbye to them, they gave me two dinars. They were really fine young men."

The third policeman added sadly, "I don't know what's got into you all. It's a curse. I know it's a curse that's descended on this land."

□

The patrol wagon passed through the night, taking streets that looked extremely beautiful to me—as if I was seeing them for the first time. I thought: Surely it's my arrest that makes them so beautiful. Through the bars of the patrol wagon I began to gaze at the pedestrians, some of whom stopped and stared at me. I made no attempt to divert my eyes from theirs. In a certain way I felt proud to be a dangerous man, even if I had done nothing to merit arrest. Other passersby smiled and whispered to each other. I had no idea what they were saying about me . . . about us . . . but attempted to guess their thoughts. They were with me in any case, even though all I really cared about was freeing myself from this morass.

It's really hard for a person to remember details, even of things he knows well. At least I could say that's the case for me. I know things, and that's enough. If you ask me the color of my mother's eyes for example, I can't reply. I know the spirit of people I'm fond of. I know the spirit of places that have been important to me. But sometimes I can't discuss the things that mean the most to me, and I'm agitated as if a storm were raging deep inside me. When I'm brooding about some cause I'm involved with, it seems I'm not even considering it. A dry cloud might as well be filling my head. When I look now, I see people without really seeing them, because I'm closed in on myself like a circle. Despite the stern appearance of the policemen and my fears and banal reactions on the way to the prison, I couldn't think straight. I felt perplexed and scatterbrained—like a smokestack discharging smoke in a gale. I was annoyed and delighted at the same time by this original and unwarranted event in my life. Perhaps I thought I might befriend some new people. These would be inevitable friendships, because I would be a prisoner too. Perhaps I thought it was a novel adventure. I smoked as calmly as a mule plodding around a gristmill. In the beginning I had felt terrified. Like any other sensation, this disappeared in time, and my mind was filled with deeds and events that are hard to imagine. I pictured myself (even if it was a joke) as a new victor entering cities of cement and steel—like an ancient world conqueror—while colored confetti showered down on me from balconies and rooftops. Here, although I was being choked by unknown fingers, I felt as cheerful as if I were in the woods. I don't know why. Perhaps if I had understood the secret, my delight and fear would both have disappeared. While I was examining my emotions (a raging river through rocky ground where colored pebbles had collected in the riverbed and fragrant flowers grew on the banks) I said, "It must have been the surprise. Here my whole world changes without any effort on my part." I thought: What hope can be based on a world that revolves within a circle? The circle was crumbling, but its destruction wasn't any real consolation for me, because the circles that surround us always require demolition.

Inside the circle, I dreamed like a weeping, deserted child. What if the patrol wagon turned over now? I didn't want to die, but a few bruises would suffice to facilitate my release. They would take me to the hospital remorsefully, regretting what I had endured. I would tell the doctor everything. He would certainly be a fine man. He would tell me, "That's true. You must go free. It's wrong for an innocent man to be imprisoned." The doctor would be gone for an hour, two hours, and then three. I would lose hope, but he would return the next day, very happy. He would tell me, "There's hope." He wouldn't want to overwhelm me with the surprise. Then at last he would laugh and tell me, "Okay. You're free. They've finally discovered their error. Put your clothes on and wait for them. They'll come soon to apologize." I would tell him, "There's no need for an apology. They just suspected me and then discovered the truth. That's what's important to all of us."

◨

The patrol wagon advanced down a dark side alley lined by towering eucalyptus trees. It stopped at a closed iron gate, which had only a small square opening in the middle. The deputy lieutenant, who had been sitting with the driver, got out and called to the policemen inside the wagon, "Wait! I'll be right back."

The policeman sitting near me stood up and replied, "Yes, sir."

Meanwhile the other two continued smoking as though this was none of their business. Two of the prisoners were chatting. The first said, "We'll ask to go to Cell Block 5."

Referring to me, the other one asked, "What about this fellow who expects to be released?" Then he turned toward me and inquired, "Do you want to be with us?"

Without any hesitation I answered, "Yes. I don't know anyone here in prison."

The policeman standing inside pushed the right section of the gate with his shoulder and it swung halfway open with a loud screech. The deputy lieutenant, who had carried our papers into the prison, said to us, "In you go! Quickly!"

There was a dark corridor lit by a feeble lamp coated with dust. On the left in the corner there was a cheap bed with a few ragged blankets. The walls were splotched with faded official notices. I thought: Couldn't they organize this chaos? The handwriting was poor, and the sentences were ill-phrased and full of laughable spelling errors and grammatical mistakes. The wall was really high and reminded me of the ramparts of a historic castle. We walked down the dark corridor to a long, wide passage running in front of six cell blocks crammed with prisoners. The administrative offices were located on the opposite side of the hall. The guards who had come out to welcome us a bit sarcastically asked us to halt. Then the warden emerged from his office opposite Cell Block 3. I stood there gravely with the others, who were trading jokes with the guards because some of them had been incarcerated here before. I began to study the tall iron grille that separated the cell blocks from the open passage. On the roofs stood a number of armed guards, who gazed down at us affectionately. When I glanced back, I saw a rotund man whose giant physique was decked in blue civilian clothes and whose pencil-thin mustache draped down from his nostrils. I guessed that he was the warden. His deputy, who wore a sharp uniform, accompanied him. Addressing the prison guards, he called out loudly, "Have you finished examining them?"

The sergeant on duty was a country fellow with a thick mustache and a comic appearance. He replied, "Yes, sir. They want to go to Cell Block 5."

The prison warden stared at us and said rather pompously, "It doesn't matter to us where you are. In fact, we prefer for you to be with your group so you don't cause us any more headaches. All I ask is for you to understand prison rules. We're not responsible for your arrest. You've been brought to us, and we're obliged to care for you till you're released or transferred to another prison."

The sergeant turned toward us and said, "I'll read your names, one by one, and each man who hears his name should pick up his belongings and step forward."

He began to call out the names: "Ahmad Husayn Salman!"

"Yes."

He placed his bedding on his left shoulder and walked away from us. He was a young man who seemed about nineteen. He wasn't especially concerned and reacted as nonchalantly to the order as if he were at home. In his right hand he carried a small green leather suitcase. He disappeared down the long passageway.

"Isam Kamil!"

"Yes."

A scrawny man in his forties, he looked tired. He must have left behind a loving wife and children. Even so, he

6

hastily picked up his possessions and rushed toward Cell Block 5, which I hadn't seen yet. Then I heard the sergeant call, "Mahmud Sa'id!"

It's my name. It's not my name. I said anxiously, "That's my name, but not exactly."

The warden laughed and asked, "What are you saying, young man? Come here."

"That's not my name. There's been some mistake. My name is Aziz Mahmud Sa'id, not Mahmud Sa'id. That's my father's name."

After taking the roster from the sergeant's hand, the warden said, "That's the only name here. It must be your name. Don't waste our time. If you have any objection, lodge it later. Now we need to sign the memo certifying your arrival."

I started grudgingly down the passage that my two mates had previously taken.

The warden called to me, "Why aren't you taking your belongings?"

I turned toward him and said, "I have nothing with me. They picked me up at a café, no doubt by mistake. . . ."

The warden interrupted me, "Fine. Fine. You can join your group."

I found Ahmad and Isam standing at the gate of Cell Block 5, waiting for the others. Standing beside them, clad in pajamas, was another prisoner who shook my hand and said, "We'll have everything prepared for you shortly."

Smoking drunkenly, I stood there with them, waiting for the others to arrive, while some inmates collected behind the gate to Cell Block 5 and began to scrutinize us through the small hole in the middle of the iron gate, which was painted black.

Two

There were feeble lights in the wide courtyard that extended to the wall separating us from the cells. In the left corner of the cell block several small trees were surrounded for their protection by a crude dirt bench. These handsome saplings were everyone's garden. Near the coffee-house, which consisted of a room that wasn't entirely enclosed, were the latrines, which lacked partitions. Inmates would sometimes continue heated discussions or exchange morning greetings and occasionally cigarettes while answering the call of nature. In the right corner, just in the middle, was the kitchen, which could be characterized as the most important and most dangerous place in the prison. Reached from the main yard—near the gate—there was another courtyard, on either side of which were a number of cells for dangerous prisoners and others for trusties. There were five other cell blocks arranged on either side of Cell Block 5, which was the largest.

At first the situation seemed a bit awkward—as if I had crashed a party hosted by strangers—so at the beginning I tried to keep out of sight in a corner, satisfying myself with surreptitious glances at the other prisoners. Scattered here and there were circles of three or four men who squatted on the ground beneath a calm, autumn sky. A refreshing breeze stirred, filling bodies with happiness. In the areas near the walls of the building and the cells, some inmates slept soundly, undisturbed by the voices of the others. From a speaker attached to a wall, I heard trite love songs repeated endlessly. A young man I reckoned to be twenty-four was engrossed in reading a large book by the light of a feeble electric lamp. I leaned against a wall, watching everyone with limitless alienation. I fixed my gaze on two men who were pacing back and forth, talking with great enthusiasm. They must have been sharing some betrayed hope. I wondered how many pains lurked beneath these serious faces. I must have been quite wrong, though, because soon they laughed heartily while continuing their evening promenade together at the same pace.

▣

Salam, who appeared to be thirty-five, headed toward me. He was the person who had provided me with two blankets, a pillow, and a pair of pajamas, since I hadn't brought any of the things I would need in prison. He told me, "You must be thinking. Don't think. Everything will be okay."

I marked his words, feeling ashamed. "No, I wasn't thinking. I was just watching the people here."

"They're fine, simple-hearted young men. You'll really like them."

"Have they been here a long time?"

"Not all of them. Some have been imprisoned for a couple of years, and others are waiting to be sentenced. There are some students and workers who have been imprisoned for two months. Some of their comrades were recently freed."

He was speaking in a very relaxed, straightforward manner. I took a chance and asked him, "Do you think I may be here long?"

Smiling, perhaps at my naiveté, he replied, "That's likely, but why consider the matter simply from this angle? You're here, and that's all there is to it. You need to adjust and accept this reality."

I responded candidly, "But I find that difficult. I must get out of here."

I was on the verge of tears. The man felt my anguish and said, "Come. Let's drink some tea."

We drank our tea standing rather than sitting on the metal drums that the convicts had turned into stools. The tea server, who was an inmate too, said, "I make the best tea here."

Salam commented with a laugh, "He makes that claim to avoid other chores like cooking, washing up, and sweeping."

The tea server laughed too and replied, "New buddy, don't fret. You'll get to try these jobs yourself."

I was enraged by this stale joke and struggled to control myself. How could this creature, who had committed I knew not what revolting crime, allow himself to address me like this? Fine, he wants to reduce me to working in the coffee-house or kitchen. That will never happen. I've been thrown into prison without committing any offense. They would have to bear that in mind.

□

I had been sitting there, at the front of the café, watching people pass by in the streets. I had come from Kirkuk to Baghdad to spend my vacation after a demanding year of work. I was thinking of finding a prostitute who would agree to take me home with her for the night, so we could sleep there together until morning. I was picturing a blissful evening, but my daydream was nipped in the bud. Yusuf, a colleague I shared an office with, had told me that the Night Town café was swarming with pimps: "Don't ask anyone. Just sit down and order tea. Then they'll throng around you, freely offering their goods." Since I was dying for a woman, I sat there for more than two hours, but no one approached me. As a matter of fact, I was prepared to sit there for hours more in order to make contact with a woman who would bring light to my tormented heart and erase the gloom of an entire year of oppressive office work. I waited for a long time without anything happening to attract my attention. Only once did I see a man look at me. I smiled at him, but he averted his face, and I felt embarrassed. All the same I was determined to wait for the arrival of the pimps who would pave the way for my nocturnal bliss. Suddenly I found myself encircled by policemen, who were surrounding the café's patrons. A policeman grabbed me by the shirt collar and told me, "Come here, mighty mouse."

I tried to say something in my own defense, but the words died on my lips. What could I say in such an awkward situation? Another policeman slapped me hard and said, "I recognize him. He's one of them."

Some patrons of the café gathered around us while others attempted to slip out another door, although the police caught them before they could escape. For some moments I thought they had mistaken me for a pimp. What rotten luck! What could I do to save myself from this dilemma? Should I tell them that I simply wanted to hook up with a prostitute? I tried to say

11

something, but a policeman dragged me out and tossed me into a large vehicle with some other people. The wagon shot off with us before we could even pay for the tea we had received.

◫

Night was filling the penitentiary. I withdrew morosely from the coffeehouse, heading for my bed in the large, dark cell near the kitchen. Two inmates were playing chess and another— leaning against the wall—was reading. Meanwhile a youth of eighteen was writing something, perhaps a letter, on his pillow, which he was using as a desk. I thought the best way I could spend this unusual night, which might be repeated many times, was to observe these men I was forced to befriend. I had no other choice. I was cast among them, and that meant I needed to win their favor. But I should never forget for a moment that my basic goal was to win my release from prison in the shortest time possible. Then what would await me in Baghdad? Hours wandering the streets, a hunt for a woman who would make me feel alive for at least one night, and then a return to Kirkuk to continue my monotonous job. I wouldn't tell my mother or any other members of my family that I'd been arrested. It would upset them a lot to discover the pain consuming me, and in return, they would only be able to offer me more tears, which I didn't need. I leaned back, deliberately banging against the wall, and stretched my legs out over the two blankets that reeked of dust and creosote. The boy who had been writing rose and walked over me as if stepping over a corpse cast out in the open air. He didn't look at me, but I gazed at his marble neck by the light from the two lamps hanging on opposite walls. I watched him pass through the open doorway to the yard. He must have grown tired of writing and sitting in a room that wasn't his own. It was a communal room, and thus no one's.

I heard one of the chess players say, "You've lost again."

"Yes, my losses keep growing, but I've not despaired of winning, even though luck's always on your side."

"But I'm a better player."

"Let's get out of this damn room."

When they passed me, they turned. One of them—a young man of about twenty-five who wasn't bad looking—asked, "How are you, buddy?"

"Oh! Thank you."

"Come along with us and don't think too much by yourself. Too much thought ruins the digestion."

I laughed and told him, "Thanks. I'll catch up with you in a bit."

I struggled to keep myself from thinking about the other people's world, the world that seemed a confusing puzzle I didn't really understand. That was why I had attempted to cut myself off from it. It had seemed to me like a dream that I shouldn't cling to for long. To provide myself with a reason to live, I found my missing happiness within myself. I would spend many hours each day alone. For a long time I had accustomed myself to sleeping during the day and staying awake by night so that no one would intrude on my private worlds. Whenever anyone dared to leap over the fences I had erected around myself, I was infuriated and clenched my teeth, suppressing my anger to avoid revealing my secret. I was sitting, looking at nothing, and thinking about ways to destroy this suspect world. I was asking myself: why do I have to accept these mistakes? But what can a prisoner like me do, far from his family, wearing torn pajamas, without even a file in the police records? All the same, I don't feel any shame. The world I'm living in can't make me feel at all ashamed. Disgrace actually envelops the peaks of the world itself: the disgrace of its silence and the inhumanity of its forgetfulness vis-à-vis the emotions of those dying in silence.

After I was taken by force from the café, the policeman sitting beside me said threateningly, "You all have ruined the world. You must pay the price."

I asked myself: Am I really responsible for ruining the world? The fault has always been there. There's some inherent defect in this world, and I'm not responsible for it. I also understood very well that the police weren't responsible for it either. No more were the leaders and scholars. I knew that the world rested on a secret flaw, but I was incapable of grasping it.

I naively asked the policeman, "But what have I done to deserve arrest?"

He answered, "Don't you know? Fine. We'll have you tell us that when we arrive."

The policeman's answer seemed baffling to me, because I wasn't certain at that moment whether I hated the authorities or loved them. They weren't my concern. The only thing I was really sure of was that I wasn't a pimp. The worst thing was that I didn't know whether I'd been arrested on suspicion of being a pimp or as an anti-government subversive.

I told myself: Never mind. I can't stay cooped up forever. I must get out and return to my job. I don't want to saunter through the streets again buffeted by crazy desires.

I stretched an arm out in front of me and rose, slipping from the communal room into the night that awaited me in the yard with the two young men who had been playing chess only a short time before.

14

Three

"The revolution is gaining ground. The wave of terror unleashed by its enemies is only the last phase of their resistance. It's true we're currently prisoners, but it's very likely that all this will be over soon. We mustn't bend before the storm. We must resist. This is what our people expect of us in this difficult stage."

Salam Abdullah, who was holding forth in the second small room on the left with some other inmates, paused. Everyone was listening to him with awe and respect. He must be a great political theorist. But how did all that concern me? I hated political games, even if I felt fond of this slender man. I was just listening. They had asked me to attend a meeting, telling me that someone wished to address us. I sat smoking with the others, relishing the celebratory air that dominated the room. I had nothing to lose. I'm a good listener. That's what they wanted. What I wanted was to leave far behind me this stone fortress, where sentries stood on the walls with their rifles, treating us to fraternal smiles as we occasionally tossed them oranges, apples, or sometimes money.

"We are not alone here. Our whole people stand beside us. They are with us night and day. Even inside the torture rooms."

How delightful! I hadn't thought about that before. Did the people really stand beside me in my isolation? In my sorrow? In my hope? But I wasn't political. What it boiled down to was that I had loitered in a café for more than two hours while waiting to locate a pimp. Then I had been arrested. That was all there was to it.

Salam turned toward me and asked, "Was your interrogation rough?"

"They didn't interrogate me. No one has spoken to me since I was arrested."

"This isn't unusual."

I explained, "There were four of us, and they addressed some questions to the three others. Then suddenly something happened. Perhaps it was something important. So they hastily brought us back. Then two days later they transported us here. That must have been an accident. I attempted to attract their attention by yelling, 'I'm innocent!' and demanding to be released, or at least interrogated, but one of the interrogators was upset by my screaming and spat in my face. He said, 'We don't have time for a trivial person like you.' No one beat me, but a rustic janitor who worked there surprised me when I entered the room and landed a kick on my butt, and the guards laughed."

For clarification, Salam Abdullah said, "They brought you in with the men distributing leaflets. Were you one of them?"

"No way. I was sitting in a café when policemen raided the place. I don't know whether any leaflets had actually

16

been distributed any more than I know why I was arrested, because no one asked me anything. All I know is that one of the men they arrested with me in the café told me later that they had distributed leaflets attacking the government. But I wasn't one of them."

"That doesn't matter. It doesn't matter. There are many innocent men here."

"But I'm not political. Why would they arrest a person like me?"

Trying to lighten the impact of the affair, Salam smiled and said, "That's true, but what's important is for you to adjust to life here first of all. So long as you're here with us, you'll continue to be one of us in every respect until you leave. It doesn't matter whether you're affiliated with us. What it amounts to is that we are confronted by an abnormal situation and mustn't succumb to it. We must sustain our human fraternity and wait."

◘

'Waiting.' This harsh word penetrated the heart like a razor-tipped harpoon. Here I was watching myself as if I were an actor seeing himself on the screen along with other members of the audience. I was almost exiled from myself. I felt lost. My destiny had escaped from me the way a fish escapes from the hands of a fisherman. Perhaps I wasn't a skillful fisherman. But did I have a fisherman's freedom of choice?

I'm just a small fish inside the net of destruction. Here I am floundering, searching for a hole that will allow me to reach the vast river that stretches away endlessly. That is my empire; without it I can't exist. I pace the dirt yard, alone, addicted to thought and observation. I wonder what kind of justice cast me into this political prison. Do you suppose I was really guilty without being aware of it? God must somehow be expressing His displeasure with me for going to a café in hopes of getting a prostitute. God had punished me for a passing fancy that I had shared with no one. I watch my feet move toward the wall until I hit it, then I turn like a blind donkey until I collide with another wall at the end of the yard. These were the only paths granted to me by munificent night and day. Thank God I was still able to perform this automatic circuit. It was the best project I could undertake in any case.

Here the policeman standing in front of his wooden shelter on the walkway atop the wall was watching and smiling at me. I returned his smile. My God, how could a person become a policeman? I have often considered almost any career in the world except policeman. But this policeman watching me with his rifle seemed very happy. He was free, and that was a huge boon. I was padding around inside a locked cage while the policeman smiled with a sweetness I did not possess.

❏

Through the middle of the day I sat near the garden to watch the inmates bending over to wash stacks of dishes as though on an endless journey. No one had asked me to perform any chore yet. I simply downed my food with four friends, since we constituted a group. One of them took charge of fetching the brass plates and then returned them afterward. Thus I spent most of my time amusing myself by watching the others. A prisoner can't keep himself from brooding, although in prisons thinking is considered a bad habit because it can lead to a spiritual collapse and to digestive and mental maladies. For this reason, prisoners combat this odious habit in various ways. When you're leaning against the wall or stretched out in bed, the first person who notices you there approaches and deliberately engages you in a long debate about any topic, no matter how trivial. There are other methods to help a man forget: playing chess, for example, learning a foreign language, or volunteering to work in the coffeehouse or the kitchen. But none of these methods interested me because I always wanted to be alone. My daydreams allowed me to feel I was creating my own private world that no one could assail.

While I watched these hardworking men, who continued their lives in prison with enviable satisfaction, I thought about the streets adjacent to the penitentiary and all the happy people who had *not* been mistakenly transported to prisons. Oh, what inane luck! I, on the other hand, was this silent guy leaning against a dusty wall—a wrong number plucked from among hundreds of thousands of people and brought shackled to the penitentiary quite simply and without any resistance. I wondered whether justice had ever existed in this strange world. Justice did not need to have anyone unveil its visage to disclose it to every eye, because it existed inside my head, in my countenance, and in my heart. It was me, precisely me, who sought deliverance in the middle of a bloodbath. The most bizarre thing about the matter was that justice did not find itself except in injustice. I had wanted them to restore my self-respect, to apologize to me, so I could emerge into the world I had lost in one fell swoop. Had they done that, however, I would have thought that justice truly existed, despite all the clamor I had heard about the death of justice in the new herd-like civilization, where everyone is a stray ewe.

A scrawny hand that might have been a twig reached toward my face, holding out a cigarette. I raised my head as if awakening from a profound dream. I accepted the cigarette. He struck a match for me. It was a fellow I had recently met in the penitentiary.

I wasn't fond of him but needed him all the same, the way I needed the wall supporting me and these men who smiled at me while they washed the pots with an earnestness that I lacked. Why do you suppose they took such pains? No answer was ready on my lips, but nonetheless I thought they had turned the penitentiary into their lost home. It was their home—not mine.

He sat down near me and said, "They brought in three new guys."

"Where are they?"

"They're in the administration and will arrive shortly."

"How unlucky!"

"Let's go peek at them through the hole in the gate."

"I don't want to. We'll see them soon enough."

The saplings swayed a little in the wind as a gray sparrow with black spots soared overhead, following an elliptical trajectory before it buzzed the guardhouse on the wall. It lit on a wooden projection near the mouth of a rifle that leaned against the wall of the room. The policeman was nowhere to be seen. Voices were audible from the far side of the wall. Perhaps the guard was also taking a look at the new prisoners, whose names were being recorded in the roster by one of the guards. The prisoners who were working in the kitchen had just finished washing the dishes and were happily going their separate ways, laughing. The bird hopped further out on the projection, where it stayed for awhile. Then it lit on the rifle's mouth, as if it were a gray rose. I felt that the rifle had been transformed. It was no longer a lethal weapon, and its greased coffee color didn't frighten me anymore. It looked like a toy in the hand of a child playing on a vast, sandy beach. No doubt this black-spotted bird felt the chill of the steel on which it was perched. In the distance I heard the cell block gate wail as it opened. The new inmates had arrived. The sparrow was startled and flew off. I felt a profound grief.

⊡

I was pacing around the courtyard when I heard a loud cry at the gate. It was my name. They were calling me. I quickly thought they must finally have come to set me free. Their mistakes would be forgiven then. All I dreamed of now was leaving these walls that oppressed the soul.

One of the men standing nearby chided me, "They're calling you. Hurry!"

I was overwhelmed by a pervasive joy when I stood before the guard who had come to summon me. I wasn't conscious any more of individual faces. Everyone had dissolved into clustered masses. I heard their flood of sentences and their scattered words, but paid no attention.

The policeman asked, "Are you Aziz Mahmud Sa'id?"

"Yes, I am."

"Fine. Come with me."

An inmate commented, "Someone must have come to visit you."

Another said, "Perhaps they'll release him."

I smiled as I went out through the gate for the first time since I'd entered. I wasn't expecting anyone, because none of my friends or family members knew where I was. They must want to interrogate me. The policeman told me, "The warden has sent for you."

When I entered the office I gazed at the warden's face for a time. Then he asked me, "Are you Aziz Mahmud Sa'id?"

"Yes. I'm Aziz Mahmud Sa'id."

"Then listen. We've sent forward your petition to the responsible agencies. Don't try that again. We don't care whether you're innocent or a criminal mastermind. All that matters is that they've sent you to us. We're responsible for looking after you until your fate is decided. Understand?"

"Yes."

"Now you can return to your cell block."

I stared him in the eyes before leaving the room. I felt there was something in them I couldn't pinpoint. Then suddenly I thought: the sparrow must have returned to the mouth of the rifle once more. From the nearby streets outside the walls I heard the wind howl in the branches of the trees.

Four

I t took me long months to comprehend that I was incarcerated. My dreams had suddenly ended. Like Zoroaster, I awoke from a lengthy slumber to discover rudely and bitterly that justice does not always favor innocence. Indeed, it occasionally supports the other side and adds to the number of victims and martyrs. In the final analysis this meant one thing for me: I might rot away inside this penitentiary without anyone noticing my existence. It seemed to me that they might not release me even if they discovered their error. I felt that I was totally forgotten.

Sitting beside me in the cell, Salam told me, "Whenever one of us is released, that is considered a political case, and this applies to you as well."

"But I'm not political."

"What you believe doesn't matter. What's important is what *they* believe."

Salam was obviously correct. He obviously understood

the truth of our current situation. I protested, "But what kind of world is this! It's a world filled with errors and crimes."

I sensed that my words had stirred Salam. His face, which was burdened with the cares of more than thirty-five years, became flushed. Then he patted me on the shoulder tenderly and said, "Let's walk in the yard a bit."

When he rose, I thought: how thin he is! He resembled Giacometti's statues; I had read an amazing article about this sculptor in an old magazine I found in the hall. All the same, he gave the impression of being more full of vitality and force than anyone else. He stood like a towering tree that provided shade to all those standing on a wobbly earth. Along with the others, I was waving my shirt over my head in the night, lifting it high for the ships that passed as my voice changed to a dry scream on the small island that was Cell Block 5 (six meters by twenty-one). There was, however, no one to climb to the crow's nest to witness the suffering of a creature that did not wish to renounce happiness. I had believed throughout my life that true happiness—even transitory happiness—constituted justice in this world. Any joy, no matter how slight, approximated justice.

"A search for justice, where there is fierce combat with the enemies, is considered a surrender to history. The only justice possible is for us to win this war."

"I'm not a soldier in this war, which I've never even considered. I've imagined for a long time that people devise these wars so they can have causes to discuss. As for me, I've grown accustomed to telling myself: Everyone is right. They must all have their reasons for launching these wars."

"That's true to some degree. Everyone has his reasons. But we must understand these reasons."

"They're convinced."

"When we erase the causes, the convictions disappear. For this dream to be realized, your incarceration remains as necessary as the fall of any other accidental victim. You're like a glass tumbler that hits the hard ground and breaks. We're concerned about the glass, since it was useful in its own way, but we don't brood about justice then."

⊞

A rather old net, which was turning gray, was fastened to two wooden posts that divided the yard into two unequal sections. On either side of the uneven dirt court, a few inmates clad in pajama bottoms and sleeveless undershirts and others in their underwear—including one young man who wore only boxers—were tossing the ball back and forth over the net. The noise they made could be heard in the other cell blocks, and perhaps even on the side streets near the penitentiary.

Along the edges of this temporary court a number of men were pursuing individual hobbies. It was an exceptionally fine day. The sun had descended behind the wall to the right of the entrance. A gentle breeze fragrant with the scent of the trees continued to blow. Mustafa was seated directly beneath the radio's speaker. This old man with a wild appearance and a hard-to-read expression was fashioning a handbag from tiny colored beads. His hands moved mechanically as he sat alone on a sheet spread on the ground. He smiled from time to time at the poor players and made loud comments that were ignored. At the same time the songs from the radio caused him to wag his white beard to the right and left as if he were a small boat heading for a cliff.

The amateur players shouted zealously. In front of the latrines at the far end of the yard, some men hovered while waiting their turn. Meanwhile, the new tea server was making the rounds of the inmates, who were scattered throughout the yard and the cells. In the blue sky, white clouds were breaking up, assuming different shapes. Beneath the clouds, beside the wall, a cheerful guard encouraged the players on the sly, since the administration would not have appreciated his affectionate chuckles. For my part, I was seated on the hard ground near the wooden posts, just at the center, watching players spring at each other like convivial wild animals in the woods. At intervals I heard the wail of the huge buses grinding to a stop at their stations. I was overcome by the bizarre notion that I was at a perpetual celebration. I noticed that Salam was standing at some distance from the players, looking furious. Sparks flew from his eyes, and I realized something was wrong. My suspicions proved well founded. Salam suddenly began screaming angrily as everyone turned his way: "Stop playing!"

He rushed at one of the players and dragged him off the court. "Who gave you permission to play?"

Yusuf, who was twenty-three, asked, trembling, "What's the matter?"

"We don't allow cowards to play with our comrades."

"I'm not a coward!"

"Shut up or I'll send you to the swamp!"

Yusuf broke into tears and withdrew, disappearing into one of the cells. I rose and followed him, feeling miserable. How could a victim turn into a torturer? The angry youth was sitting calmly in a corner of the room. He might just as well have been a corpse straight from a cemetery. I sat down close

26

to him and said, "I'm sorry about what happened. Salam committed an offense for which I'll never forgive him."

Yusuf looked at me and said, "You mustn't think about it. It doesn't concern you."

"It does too concern me."

"You'll be ostracized then."

"That doesn't matter."

"Fine. Then you need to know the truth. Salam wanted to humiliate me because of what I said in court. Like many others, I may receive a harsh verdict. I'm not afraid, not even of death. All it amounts to is that I wanted to be true to myself and my ideas. The judge asked whether I support assassination as a political tool. Instead of replying with the formula that the leadership imposed on us—I have no opinion on this subject and know nothing about it—I made it clear that I oppose crimes and that every crime, no matter what rationale justifies it, must be condemned. I wasn't afraid. I wished to say what I believe."

The tea server entered, glared at me spitefully, and then said, "Salam has summoned you. He wants to talk to you."

I thought I wouldn't go, but Yusuf said, "Go on."

"I can't bear to see his face."

"That would be dangerous for you. Go on, and don't defend me."

When I stood up, he gazed at me and smiled, saying, "Please."

◫

Salam told me, "I'm as sad as you are about what happened, but it was necessary. We need to be steadfast, otherwise we're finished. Our strength resides in the courageous stands we take, and we can never be too harsh."

27

What could I say? Other men were sitting near Salam. They had their eyes on me. They must be thinking something. Had I too committed a crime that deserved to be punished? But what was that to me? I was the inmate who had committed no offense. I wasn't one of them, even though I was housed with them. It was all the same to me whether I was with them or in some other location so long as my freedom was attached to the end of a rope of unknown length.

I said a bit boldly, "I don't want to meddle in your affairs, but as a person who understands little about politics, I feel public denunciation is a harsh punishment that could push him to an even worse position."

Salam smiled sarcastically, "We don't care if we lose the cowards. All we want from you is to stay away from him and avoid him. Everyone will break with him. No one will speak to him. We want him to feel our total contempt for the position he adopted in court. If he changes his opinion in the coming session, then our treatment of him may change."

"You're asking something impossible of him. Should he tell the court: 'Sorry, I misstated my opinion the last time with respect to politically motivated murders. I don't condemn them, because I have no opinion about them.' This is crazy and also harsh, very harsh."

Salam responded coldly, "We all proceed harshly. Weren't you brought to prison from a café without ever committing a crime? Personal opinions don't count. The last thing that interests them is the answer and its meaning. They simply want to humiliate anyone the fates lead to their courts. We must confront their harshness with even greater harshness."

The night was beautiful, but not for Yusuf, who had been banished to the swamp—a dilapidated cell that had been left deserted until inmates transformed it into a prison within a prison. The door was opened only three times a day, and food was provided to the residents through a small hole in the door. No one was allowed to talk with them. To this room near the latrines were sent people whom other inmates normally called traitors and scum. Yusuf did not protest when they moved him there. His bedding on his shoulders, he carried away his possessions as silently as a calm sea. I was standing near the swamp room when Yusuf passed. I really wanted to smile at him from a distance and encourage him, but he totally ignored me and joined his other colleagues who had been condemned to the swamp. The swamp cell was a secret to no one. It was a fact of life accepted even by the prison's administrators, who preferred not to intervene in the inmates' private affairs, provided that order and calm prevailed. They actually preferred to keep a safe distance from anything that would rile the inmates, who constituted a society apart with its own systems, tribunals, and administration. Here ended the external world, which was no longer anything more than a dream comparable to the dreams of those contemplating a trip to Paris, London, or any other distant city.

That evening, Isam, the tea server, came to me once he finished work and said, "They're angry at you."

Isam's comment upset me, and I studied him. Closing the door on my other thoughts, I asked, "Who?"

"The others."

"But why? What have I done?"

"They don't know anything about you and say you may be a police plant. Yet you continue to interfere in their affairs."

"That's utter nonsense."

"You followed Yusuf after he was ostracized and then consoled him."

"You spied on me. You all were playing ball with him yourselves moments before."

"That was a trap we set for him. We wanted to humiliate him in front of everyone."

I felt like cursing him but chose to remain silent. Fine, I'm not one of them. Perhaps I don't even have a right to express my opinion. Even so, I felt that all this should change. I was upset to see one victim torturing another. It had to change. I had to work to put an end to it. But how? I thought that misery might be man's destiny everywhere but that the heavens weren't responsible for it. It was our own doing; the blame belonged to all human beings throughout history.

All night long I wept silently on my two blankets that were too thin to prevent bumps in the floor from poking into various parts of my body. I no longer cared about anything, not even about being released. I mourned for all human beings with a lethal grief. I sank ever deeper into an infinite stupor, a stupor of the human heart.

Five

I rested my notebook against the pillow. I was thinking of writing a brief letter to my mother, even though I knew she would have palpitations when she learned I had been arrested. But there was no getting around it. My disappearance would cause her even more sleepless nights. Unless I revealed the truth to her, she would think I had died or quit the country, leaving her on her own. I thought of writing a second letter to a colleague in the office where I worked, but abandoned that idea. I felt sure that they would take steps to terminate me contemptuously if they learned I had incriminated myself in a political case. I knew them very well—better than they did themselves. I would become a story they told their wives before falling asleep. My sudden disappearance like this, however, would merely give them a headache. They would reflect a great deal—a thousand times over—racking their brains, without ever arriving at a satisfactory answer. Once I'm released and return to them, I'll find enough justifications for my absence that it won't be hard to obtain normal or compensatory dispensation for the months spent in prison.

Mun'im, who slept beside me, approached and asked, "What are you writing?"

"I'm writing a letter to my mother."

"Do you have to?"

"Yes. She'll be anxious."

"But she doesn't know. That's better."

I smiled at Mun'im, who had become my friend recently. I began to write.

Dear Mother,

I hope my absence hasn't worried you. I've been forced to stay in Baghdad for a time I believe will be short. The cause for my delay—I hope this won't upset you—is that I'm currently under arrest. This resulted from a misunderstanding. They realize now that I'm not the person they want, but my release will take some time. I have enough money and don't need anything. All I want from you is not to be anxious, for I'm spending lovely, blissful days. Don't tire yourself with coming to visit me, because I may be freed at any moment. I also hope you won't tell my brother Ahmad about this, especially since he's experienced acute psychological problems recently. I know that you are very strong and capable of coping with problems courageously. That's why I'm writing you.

With my love and greetings,

Aziz

Baghdad, Penitentiary, Cell Block 5

When I finished writing the letter, I asked Mun'im, "Do you have a mother?"

He laughed and replied, "I'll introduce you to my family on visiting day."

"I don't like families very much. They remind me of prison."

"You'll change your mind this time."

Mun'im, a university student studying English literature, had been arrested approximately two months earlier—after participating in a student demonstration. He was a young man of twenty-two with a tawny complexion. His indifference to spending time in prison while his friends continued their studies astonished me. As a matter of fact, he too was studying, but in his own way. He had books piled by his head, and it seemed to me that he was combating imprisonment by reading. When I mentioned that to him, he said, "Prison's not as bad as people make out. It's actually a rare opportunity for us to spend time alone and to reflect on the social freedom we've lost. Can you read a book a day outside prison? That's almost impossible. But in prison, you can read more than ten books a week. People in our era are totally bereft of reason and oblivious to themselves. Life's monotony is harsher outside, where man falls prey to his multiple relationships. In prison, a man can retrieve all his life's lost opportunities. Oh, how long I've dreamed of changing my life in some respects— disappearing, for example. On solitary nights when I was alone, I would think about withdrawing to a cave in a forest the way ancient holy men did, but I never had the chance. Only in prison have I discovered the strength to realize this dream. I'm truly happy, really happy."

Mun'im excited me. He seemed very strange. He wasn't like the others. While they spoke and behaved in a disgustingly

33

dead fashion, Mun'im excited me with his ideas, language, and novel actions. It was as if a continent had risen from the ashes of hundreds of stagnant seas. Although he was with them, he still wasn't one of them. His ideas were out there in another world, where a man wouldn't be killed or scorned. A new freedom exploded from the emotions of people confronting death at every moment. The image of the revolution in his head didn't resemble that of the others. He opposed all crimes, without regard to their justification. He told me one day, when we were strolling around the prison yard, "If a single crime's committed, it can mar the revolution's beauty. I dream of a beautiful revolution."

I retorted, "But mistakes are inevitable."

He looked at me petulantly and said, "You've started to turn into one of them. People who combat the world's errors do not err."

He was silent for a time. Then he asked, "Do you believe that Salam is trustworthy?"

I replied hesitantly, "I don't know."

"Fine. I know this type of impostor, the convulsive hero who doesn't hesitate to commit any offense to safeguard his hegemony that fills an internal void. Perhaps Yusuf's stance in court didn't agree with Salam's, but that doesn't give him the right to denounce, suppress, and torment him a second time. Salam is no less brutal than the judge who interrogated Yusuf."

I said, "Do you realize that ideas like these could land you in the swamp?"

He laughed and replied, "The swamp's no more putrid than justifying crimes. The swamp doesn't frighten me, but they won't be able to send me there. They normally do that only to weak people who are unable to fight back. As for me, it's all the same whether I live or die. For that reason, they prefer to leave me alone and to humor me at the same time."

"I feel lost."

"Feeling lost is the beginning of the road."

The next day, thrilling news spread among the penitentiary's residents. The prisoners in the swamp had begun a hunger strike. No one dared to speak openly about this strike, which could raise a lot of issues with the administration, although everyone was whispering about it. What did the swamp prisoners want? Their one demand was to be released from their second jailhouse inside the penitentiary. The two other men in the swamp—Husayn and Salman—had spent more than twenty days without books, paper, or even a chess piece. They hadn't seen the sun throughout this period except when they were permitted to visit the latrines before returning to their dilapidated cage.

Salman was a railroad worker arrested on charges of political agitation. Husayn had been a teacher in a southern village, where he was accused—at the instigation of one of the feudal lords who dominated the village—of propagating atheist ideas. Alleging that he was disseminating anarchist ideas, Salam sent him to the swamp. He once stood before the inmates and delivered a speech that caused all those who believed in the future's happy utopia to quake in their seats. "I know that many people die as martyrs for the sake of the truth—or what they believe to be the truth. But is there really a truth in this world? I tell you that to perceive the truth, you must stand before the world and whistle scornfully at everything: love, ethics, history, and martyrs too. Any coward, any simpleton or fool can be transformed into a hero if a stray bullet strikes him and he dies. The elite in this world are nothing but abject, self-satisfied dolts who have accustomed themselves to saying yes, even to lies. I myself am searching for the man who knows that deliverance in this world is impossible but nonetheless stands courageously before all of existence and says no."

Unlike Husayn, Salman was a wreck, a human corpse who couldn't stop crying and begging the police to work to set him free because if he stayed in jail, his wife might become a prostitute. Salam had at first spoken to him several times, but to no avail. Husayn was characterized to a large degree by a braggart anarchism, whereas Salman was a hopeless wreck who would never be able to stand on his feet again. Salam had isolated them to keep them from affecting the other inmates' morale.

Salam, who was accompanied by Abdulkareem Kazim—a short, young, obese ambulatory barrel of a man who lived in Salam's own cell—went to the swamp. The morning was still young when Abdulkareem peered into the cave and said, "Salam wants to speak to you."

A voice from inside replied, "We don't want anyone."

Salam approached the peephole and addressed his three prisoners, "This conduct seems totally depraved."

A voice issued from inside: "We're dying here."

"What can I do? You chose your fate yourselves."

"Our confinement here is inhumane."

"All we're doing is protecting ourselves from you."

A scream like a wail resounded from within, "I'm sick! Very sick!" Then it died away.

The inmates who had gathered excitedly behind Salam tried to glean every word. When Salam finished speaking with his prisoners, he turned toward the assembled inmates and asked them to disperse. Then he returned silently to his cell, while the others continued discussing the swamp's inhabitants as though they were mangy dogs deserving no mercy.

⊡

That evening, the prison committee for Cell Block 5 called a general meeting to discuss the hunger strike proclaimed by the three detainees. Although to preclude eventual judicial review the prison's administrators preferred to avoid interfering in the prisoners' affairs, they could not remain silent if the banished men continued their strike. The inmates crowded into the large room in the center. The atmosphere was tense. Flushed faces arrived to decide the fate of the three rebels. They had yet to reach any decision regarding them, but their attitude had been determined even without any prior agreement. It was a symbolic stance that took root inside all of us without our noticing. Wouldn't it have been possible for Salam and his committee to negotiate a settlement without this tense carnival? I don't know. There must have been some additional problem, because large assemblies like this were only held under exceptional circumstances. Salam sat in the middle, facing the room's open door as the other committee members— Abdulkareem, Rafi', and Sallah—pressed together beside him. Abdulkareem was smoking and smiling at the others while Rafi' and Sallah chatted. I was thinking about my sandals, which I had left in a pile with tens of others at the door. It was very likely that I would lose them, because someone else would slip into them and walk off, forcing me to search for them in front of the other cells and on everyone's feet. I thought I ought to get up and stuff them into my pocket, but felt embarrassed. This conduct might induce all the others to mock me—the person who was the mistaken name in the police files.

Salam had begun to speak: "Things among us have become really bad and must be returned to normal. Discipline is the one reality that can guard us against the authorities' oppression. You must know that we live in total comfort in comparison with our comrades who live in other prisons and penitentiaries. In Ba'quba Prison, for example, prisoners are brutally beaten and their heads are shaved. They are also prohibited from writing letters to their relatives. We, however, are held in this penitentiary to which everyone else dreams of being transferred. We have gradually been able to pressure the administration into accepting this humane situation on which we pride ourselves. We won't allow any sabotage or tolerate it."

Salam continued his talk, but I was thinking about the row of footwear deposited by members of the audience along the wall opposite me. Inmates only wore shoes on special occasions: when heading to an interrogation or trial or when they were released. This did not mean, however, that they neglected their footwear. I had observed many shining their shoes from time to time and donning them for religious festivals, special events, and an occasional promenade in the yard when they were overwhelmed with longing to return to the tumultuous streets. They acted the same way with their old clothes, which they replaced with new ones—as if heading to a party or a wedding.

I heard Abdulkareem say, "Fine. I'll go summon them."

They were talking about the group in the swamp.

Abdulkareem set off with Rafi' while Salam continued his talk. "We're certainly not against them. But we are against political lapses and sabotage." Mun'im, who sat beside me, was reading a small book he had brought while pretending to listen, glancing at Salam's face from time to time. All eyes turned toward the door. I turned as well. The weather was cloudy, and dust filled the air, coloring it red. I felt a kind of inner dread, as if I were entering a tunnel that led to the death chamber. The three banished men stood at the door, accompanied by Abdulkareem and Rafi'. Rafi' said, "Go on in. The comrades wish to speak to you."

I knew Yusuf but had never seen the other two before. Even so I didn't need to ask who they were. I recognized the laborer Salman by his wan, exhausted face, which was washed with pallor and feebleness. Husayn looked feisty and hostile. I was amazed by his thick beard and didn't know whether he had grown it during his captivity or before.

Husayn snorted, "Fine. What do you want from us?"

Salam replied calmly, "Sit down, first of all."

Husayn and Yusuf sat down, but Salman went weeping to Salam and kissed his head. This banal gesture touched all of us. Despite his misery and inanity, we were all on his side. Salam tried unsuccessfully to dodge but was surprised by Salman's wretched kiss. Finally Salman collapsed on the ground like a wounded victim who awaits his killer's mercy.

Rafi' regained control of the situation: "We want to talk to you."

Husayn asked defiantly, "About what?"

"You've asked to leave the swamp. Isn't that so?"

Husayn smiled sardonically. "Is there some other swamp to which you wish to send us?"

Salam intervened, "Don't make things harder, Husayn. We want to find a solution to the problem."

Salman screamed grievously, "I'm sick! Very sick! I'm with you one hundred percent. I've made a mistake. I admit I'm an insignificant, despicable person. Here, I criticize myself. What more do you want?"

Husayn said, "So you ask us to imitate this wretched conduct. You want me to criticize myself—not for any offense I've committed but to appease your uneasy consciences. Like any other man, I have my own ideas. You talk about the truth as if you had purchased it from God in person. All it amounts to is that I don't want to be a puppet in anyone's hands. Your blind belief in your truths will never make you more sincere than I am in combating injustice."

Salam retorted irritably, "You're making the situation more difficult, Husayn. Since you continue to insist on circulating sick bourgeois ideas like these, you have two choices: stay in the swamp or request transfer to another penitentiary selected for you by the police. In this case, your best choice would be an ordinary prison, because we will advise all of our imprisoned comrades to refuse to accept you among them."

Husayn said calmly, "I don't care what you think of me. That's why I'll stay in the little swamp, leaving you in your large one."

Then he rose and quit the room for the swamp.

◘

The next morning the prison administration conducted a surprise inspection. About ten guards, armed with revolvers, burst into the cell block. They were led by the prison's police supervisor, Mundhir Abduljabbar, a young man of around twenty-seven with an angry red face. I wondered what had prompted this surprise raid. Salam and Abdulkareem went out to greet them while a number of the inmates quickly hid their small radios in places the guards wouldn't think to look. These precautions, however, proved unnecessary, because the police supervisor headed straight for the swamp room and attempted to open the door, which was locked. He peered through the peephole and then told Abdulkareem, who was standing beside him, "It's true we're lenient with you, but this farce must stop."

Abdulkareem, who looked bewildered—as if he were an accomplished actor—asked, "What's the matter?"

"A lot of things. You're trying to deceive us. Isn't that so? You know very well that the three prisoners in there are on hunger strike because they've been confined to this miserable room. What would you say about us if we did that to you? You seem to yearn to be worse police than we are. What's this all about? What? Give me the key at once."

They gave him the key and he unlocked the door. The only person inside was Husayn, who told the police supervisor, "Please don't upset me by talking, because that gives me a headache."

The police officer asked disapprovingly, "You're a captive—isn't that so? They've forced you to stay in this room."

"A captive? You must be joking. I regret to inform you that your information is incorrect. I chose to withdraw to this room because I can't bear the inmates' clamor. I actually suffer from headaches."

"But my information indicates that you're on hunger strike to protest your imprisonment in this room as a result of political differences with them."

41

Husayn laughed and replied sarcastically, "Why should my political stance differ from theirs? There's not an atom of truth in what you say. I'm with them till death. I actually thank them for granting me the opportunity to enjoy the quiet here."

"Fine, if this is what you want."

Then, turning to the inmates congregating around the door, he said, "Okay. Your bizarre positions make me wonder about you. You brutally oppress someone, but when we attempt to approach him to extend a helping hand, he recoils as if we were mangy dogs. Tell me what destructive, disruptive secret lurks in your heads."

When the guards left the cell block, the door to the swamp remained open, because no one dared to lock it. Salam, who was thunderstruck by the police raid on the prison, was brooding about the stool pigeon who had leaked information to the police about affairs in the cell block.

Six

During the days following the police raid, the cell block was gloomier than before. Each pain-ridden face showed deeply etched doubt lines. The cell block had lost its previous purity because the administration had succeeded in planting spies among us. The police paid us frequent visits. They were no longer soft on us. They repeatedly summoned Abdulkareem, a member of the penitentiary council, and humiliated him within sight of us. Abdulkareem said nothing. He tried to remain calm and self-confident, even as he struggled to control his riotous emotions. Some inmates wanted to rebel against the new oppression that the prison administration had implemented, but Abdulkareem forbade that, saying, "They're trying to manipulate us. We must outwit them. We will choose the moment of battle ourselves."

The penitentiary's police supervisor reviled Abdulkareem in an unprecedented way. What was happening? No doubt things had changed. He had been a fine man and then had changed into a savage beast.

"They must have received some new directives from their superiors."

The police supervisor's face flushed as he addressed Abdulkareem, "You all don't seem to deserve our respect. We've tried to treat you like human beings, but you've rejected that."

The police supervisor disappeared through the inner gate, which was locked again. The inmates were overwhelmed by a strange apprehension similar to the emotions of a drowning man who feels the weeds growing at the bottom of the river. Salam entered his cell and leaned against the wall. He stayed there smoking, without anyone daring to go near him. He must have been thinking about what he would have to do to respond to the police supervisor's provocations. Here night was returning once more, and a powerful light—a light in the desert—would be needed. The footprints that sank into the sand of the crime must form a path that would lead to the other city we all awaited—me along with the others, although I had never even had a city.

When morning came, I felt its special sweetness, for it wasn't like other mornings. Everyone had quit work. The kitchen staff didn't bother to cook. The cleaning crew didn't set out to sweep the yard or clean the cells. Even tea distribution halted. For the first time since I had entered the penitentiary, I felt like a normal person, a man in the street. The prison suddenly disappeared and faded from sight like a wave spreading over the sea's night, washing the shore's eternal sands. I looked for Mun'im everywhere in the yard but didn't find him. Eventually I came across him inside the bedroom. He was shaving. I sat on the edge of my bed to watch him. The mirror rested against an empty box, and he sat before it, bending over, examining his face. At least ten other men were leaning over their mirrors, shaving or putting on clean pajamas, exchanging jokes with barefaced delight.

"I've looked everywhere for you."

"I'm shaving, as you see. Go on and shave too. Soon I'll introduce you to my mother and my sister Salwa."

Salwa must be beautiful, since she's a university student. I wonder what will happen if I attempt to gain her affection. I don't think Mun'im would object. He's an outstanding young man who has told me for ages that political revolution alone will not suffice. There must be an overall revolution encompassing gender relations, morality, economics, and everything. What's important isn't creating a revolution, because one that doesn't include all the aspects he mentioned would be stillborn. What's important is creating a new man purified by the fire of the human revolution.

I would say, "But how? How?"

"We'll change everything."

"But people will still be the same people, even during a revolution. We won't be able to rent another population."

"The fault cannot lie with the people. It must lurk in the existing institutions, which we must destroy, and in the class structure, which dupes people. We must blaze a trail to happiness through a fiery desert."

"It'll be a harsh desert."

"That's the only possible price."

"What comes after that?"

"We'll be less miserable."

◫

I wasn't expecting anyone I knew—no one to whom I was linked by enduring emotions. People we know quickly succumb to the law of custom, taking the easy way out. Benign fraternal forgetfulness holds them captive. My personal relations with the entire world were more or less kaput—perhaps because of the mistake the policeman had made when he escorted me to prison. Included were all those I had known in the past— in coffeehouses and offices, on the streets. I had forgotten them the way a man occasionally forgets what his own face looks like. They were with me, in my head, but merely as cadavers I preserved like mummies. The previous night I had thought I would stay out of sight today and not venture into the other yard to see the visitors—that would be normal for me—because I'm a forsaken person who waits for no one. But I went out now, dragging my feet, to the people arriving from all the neighborhoods of this city, which lay entombed in my memory, and from other faraway cities I didn't know. My excuse was that I wanted to meet Salwa and that I had promised Mun'im, who wished me to be there.

There were women in abayas and radiant, chic girls who reminded us of the magic of the other life outside the penitentiary. Men played with their children, crones stared at inmates' faces, and barefoot village women lamented bitterly. My heart was filled with pain. What emotions these people carried to us! They increased our feeling of loss even as we expected them to bring our hearts the springtime they lacked. Some laughed too.

46

I listened to the melancholy conversation of a loving couple. The woman said, "I don't let a day pass without going to the bridge where we used to walk each evening. I go alone, because I don't want anyone to see me. I stand at the middle of the bridge and cast a single rose into the river. That's your rose."

"Soon I'll be with you so we can cast our roses together."

I left the lovers to search for Mun'im, who was also staring at faces, searching for me in order to introduce me to his family. He pulled me by the elbow and said, "Come. Don't be embarrassed!"

She stood there encouragingly—as radiant as dawn over a river. It was the very river that sweeps away in its passage all the filth accumulated in the world. No girl could be so gracious. She was the river that I had been struggling to reach all my life. She smiled encouragingly at me as Mun'im's hand squeezed my elbow as if to tell me, "See how beautiful my sister is!"

Mun'im said, "This is Salwa, whom I've mentioned."

Addressing Salwa, I asked, as I drowned in the blue of her eyes, "How are you, Salwa?"

She shook her head gently, causing her long hair to flutter in the wind. "You must be Aziz. I feel I know you completely. Mun'im has told me a lot about you in his letters."

Mun'im's mother looked up at us and said fondly, "Let's sit down, for we're all one family."

How I wished I really was a member of this family! The mother was somewhat sad about our fate. Salwa was oblivious to all that. Unlike the others, she made no attempt to speak to us as if we were lost souls or to shower us with affection—that gratuitous affection that brought us nothing but more sorrow.

Mun'im said, "You keep her busy so I can talk with my mother a bit."

I gazed at Salwa moodily and she asked, "Do you feel sad?"

"At first I was very sad. Now it doesn't much matter to me. I seem to be adjusting to my new life."

"You must resist that feeling. The one thing linking you to the world is your sense that you will emerge to the street again. If you lose this feeling, you will have lost yourself."

"But the world has dispensed with us. We alone pay the price for the world's errors. The others who want us to resist for their sake have fallen silent. We're no longer useful in the eyes of the others—relatives and friends, who are always busily engaged in everything we're forbidden."

Salwa said, "You're totally mistaken, because we're with you. We carry you in our hearts the way we bear our sorrow, the way we live our love. We listen to your voices at night."

Then she leaned forward gracefully and said ironically, "Do you want me to weep? Please don't make me misty-eyed."

"We want to be remembered."

She raised a hand from beneath the hem of her blouse, which fell down to her legs, and began to run her fingers delicately over her face. An electric storm convulsed me from head to foot. Those extraordinary fingers, which made me feel alive for the first time since I had entered prison, intoxicated me. Her smile was as sweet as a happy daydream. Then I heard her whisper to me, "Fine. I'm with you."

My heart was suddenly filled with overflowing love, many lights shone before my eyes, and all the way to the horizon the colors of the world became even more resplendent as my fingers clung to the grass growing on the shores and

48

I hoped to attain the city of my dreams. For the first time in my life I felt happy, though a stranger.

Like a person refusing to acknowledge his happiness, I stammered out a few phrases: "But that's impossible. You don't know me. I might be just another blockhead. It was a pure coincidence that I ended up in jail. I don't even have a cause to defend."

"That's not important. It's of no importance at all. What I feel at the moment is that you would like me to stand beside you, and I will."

I shuddered as if awakening from a deep nightmare and shouted, "I don't want pity!"

The sound of my words reached Mun'im, who turned toward me and laughed. "Salwa must have provoked you. She's a demon in a woman's body. Beware of her!"

As if issuing an order, Salwa proclaimed, "We're going to observe the prisoners a little."

I rose when she did to stroll through the yard, which was filled with visitors and inmates. Salwa remarked, "Only aged horses deserve pity."

◘

Throughout that day and those that followed, I felt tipsy from the emotions that flowed through my body. Here I found myself on close terms with an enchanting woman after I had traversed all the world's deserts alone, alienated even from the people closest to me. I was unable to accustom myself to this voice that had suddenly reached me in prison; it must be a dream that daylight would quickly disperse. I thought the whole affair had perhaps been a beguiling lie. But, amazingly, it wasn't a fantasy. Salwa had sat beside me pressing her soft leg against mine and stretching the fingers of her right hand to my face to play with my hair. I was able to waylay the truth that was diffused by her passing smile. No one would be capable anymore of separating me from this girl who had sat in my shadow, because she was my lost freedom, my recompense for the world I had accidentally forfeited. Salwa did not enlarge the prison that had closed its gates on me, nor did she end the pain I felt now. But she granted me the power to resist and to bond with other people. She had opened the pores of my skin and calmly slipped into my blood. I no longer felt alone because here I found myself inside her, united—as masterful and sorrowful as a prophet on the cross. I realized that there was someone now who thought about my destiny, and I was inundated by a wave of existential light.

◫

Yesterday they led off to court Mustafa, the farmer who dreamed of establishing the capital for his revolution in the countryside. But he did not return to us. He did not return to his corner in the yard or to his few friends who had teased him by discussing exceptional and singular topics.

"Will sex be allowed in your future capital?"

"What kind of talk is this? Do your think our struggle is to open a brothel?"

"So do you want us to marry?"

"You can stay single if you want, but I'll slay with bullets anyone who assaults a woman not his own."

Mustafa did not return to us. We waited for him till evening, when we learned that they had sent him to the "Training Room," which was a small, dark chamber, where

50

he would be all alone. I wondered whether Mustafa cared whether he was with us. Was it possible that he would feel oppressed by solitary confinement? I didn't know, but Salam, who had spent his first three months of imprisonment in solitary confinement, had once said, "After one month of the Training Room, I felt I had forgotten how people converse. I yearned to hear no matter what word or incomplete sentence that might reach me from the distance. The guard who brought my food was so careful not to move his lips that I thought he was mute. I was dying of desire for any human sound. I felt that silence like this was intolerable. One time my nerves were shot and I began to scream without stopping. When the guard stood outside my cell, I slapped him, hoping he would curse me and release some sound, but he remained silent, smiling craftily and meanly at me. During the long, boring days I talked loudly to myself or sang or acted out scenes from old school plays that still stuck in my mind. At times I delivered a zealous speech to a nonexistent throng. When night fell I would go to bed early to dream of garrulous men and women."

I wondered whether Mustafa would be able to endure the experience of isolation without scars to his spirit. I believed he would, because his harsh life in the countryside had taught him what I hadn't learned from all the books I had read. I wondered why this old farmer was being punished. Why was he placed in solitary confinement? His trial had not concluded and no verdict had been handed down in the case yet. We wanted him to return to us, but the police supervisor ruled that out, saying, "He's a very bad man."

"What did he do?"

The police supervisor laughed and replied, "All he did was throw his shoe at the presiding judge."

51

"But why? He's not crazy."

"The presiding judged asked him to confess to his crimes committed on behalf of farm workers and to ask for clemency. Instead of yielding, he pulled off his shoe and threw it at the judge's face, shouting, 'It's not possible for pimps like you to judge the revolution.'

"When they brought him back to us, his clothes were stained with blood. Apparently they had beaten him inside and outside the cage. They demanded that we teach him some manners, but he wouldn't have been able to endure any more beating and we didn't want to be responsible for his death. We thought the solution to this dilemma was to confine him inside one of the solitary cells until he was sentenced and moved to the central prison. He's a very cantankerous peasant and kept cursing us even then from his cell. He was furious with all of us."

I didn't grieve too much for him, although I missed him. Perhaps he missed all of us—this innocent revolutionary who spied a capital city that had not yet been erected. I wondered whether Mustafa had lost his capital forever. Had he lost the ticket to enter his world, which he wanted to be different from ours?

One time Mustafa asked me, "What does a job in the city offer you? Money? But what's the use of money if it costs you your liberty? Quit your jobs and head to the countryside, which lacks police, laws, tribunals, and cars speeding down streets. Go to the forests and learn to love the beasts and the trees. Only there is the paradise you futilely seek. If only you had a little bit of courage, a very little bit, you could see paradise."

If Mustafa had raised the curtain on class hatred in the city, I had discovered it in the penitentiary. There was a lovely small room next to Salam's. Completely furnished, it was nicely appointed with a kerosene stove beside the door. No outsiders went near it. In this room lived a major merchant, two attorneys, a physician, and a university professor. Everyone treated them in a special way that made me feel they were guests of honor. Their privileges, however, kindled my loathing, disdain, and resentment. Indeed, I deliberately insulted them a number of times. Even though the rest of us all ate the same food, theirs always came from restaurants. They had paid off the penitentiary guards, but only on their own behalf, and so they lacked for nothing. In a corner of the room, assorted cans were always piled high in a mound that we walked past, even though we were hungry. We heard them discuss the revolution and those weaklings who collapse under torture at the very same time that they were expecting to be freed after paying bribes—hundreds of dinars—into the police's pockets. Even so they did not offer us so much as a single glass of milk—we who were their impoverished comrades and the fuel of their future revolution. We hated them, but some loved them too. After returning from the swamp, Salman was transformed into their servant: preparing their food and washing their clothes. He ate after they did and cleaned the room, regaling them with his stale jokes. Perhaps they gave him money to send his wife and children, because he stopped complaining about penitentiary life after he found his deliverance in serving the elite.

Some referred to them fondly: "See how they sacrifice themselves for us."

Mun'im told me, "They're very clever. Once the revolution succeeds, they'll get all the glory. They are the cabinet officers of the new government."

On nights when we were hungry, Husayn would slip into their room as deftly as a cat and steal an assortment of delectable foods—canned goods, milk, cheese, and fruit that we distributed to the penitentiary's other poor, saying, "Eat. It comes from the swine's sty."

Husayn would always repeat, "I feel I wasn't created to be a teacher. I'm a far better thief than anything else."

When Salam learned about our nocturnal raids on the room of our VIP guests he laughed and said, "They provoke the nationalist bourgeoisie against us."

❐

My heart was suddenly filled with such delight that its black night turned to brightest day. Walls inside me collapsed, and my body vibrated with peace like a springtime tree blooming on a sandy hill where the dew-laden breeze and the thick fog intoxicated me. From afar, from childhood, where butterflies hovered over flower petals and the black mare crossed the field's irrigation ditch, where children gathered in front of the isolated police station located on the only street—next to the primary school—I witnessed the endless progress of my heart to a consciousness that flooded me with its memories here in this arid, desolate prison. Salwa looked down on me from the far side of the walls, telling me, "Now you too have become addicted to love like amateur thieves. See how clean things look in sudden rains!"

The rain was falling in torrents. The storm's thunder and lightning had taken us by surprise. I was stretched out on my bed—a bed of rags—gazing at the night, which was being washed by the rain. Salwa was with me too. My mother, who no longer recognized me, was there. They were both looking at me, and I was looking at the rain through the night's darkness, through freedom's vast expanse. I felt sorrowful. Nothing had happened to justify my sorrow, but I was so happy I felt sad. I borrowed a cigarette from another inmate and got up. I stood at the large room's open door. The men were busy recalling the delights of their day, which was ending. I thought I would write a daily letter to Salwa. She would tell herself, "How much this solitary man loves me!" But that wasn't enough. I would write another letter to my mother. A letter to my brother. A letter to my friends. A letter to a nonexistent man.

At the moment I felt I truly was a stranger. Why all this craziness? The people I lived with had opened a gate to another world that I had never seen before. Should I attempt to enter? What would I lose? I had lost my freedom because of an act I hadn't committed. After that, what more was there for me to fear? I actually was afraid. I wasn't like them. It wouldn't be hard for me to resemble them—I who was there among them, I who was a stranger in their midst—even though Salwa might find that comic. She might mock me—I who at that moment stood alone and thought alone and observed the rain alone.

The yard was totally empty. There was absolutely no one there. I went out to the yard and sat on a metal barrel in a corner of the darkened coffeehouse that was open to the yard. The trees were wailing like a widow or a raging river. I felt them tremble inside my body, which new emotions had dissolved. Close to the corner nearest the guardroom, a specter was moving in the dark. I focused on him. I couldn't make out his features very well. I saw him stop there and toss something toward the guardroom. What was this man of the night doing? He turned away, afraid of being seen, and cautiously glanced right and left before heading to his room. In response, I plastered myself ever more tightly against the wall. By a flash of lightning I recognized him and could make out the left side of his face. It was Abdulkareem, a member of the penitentiary committee, in person. I felt a severe tremor throughout my body, because his features hid a policeman whose mask had slipped down.

The trees wailed once more, and I returned to my narrow corner of the room, thinking about man—this creature more misguided than a caravan lost in Arabia.

Seven

Salwa said, "I often talk about you and sometimes imagine you're with me. Perhaps I'm a prisoner of my fantasies."

"Perhaps I've entertained you. Perhaps I've been just a toy you play with."

"No! Not at all! You're mistaken."

"Why?"

"Because I really find myself close to you."

"Why me? Why me of all people?"

"I don't know. Perhaps because you're more genuine than the others. I grasped that the first moment—even before we spoke."

"But I'm not genuine. I don't know if there really is a single genuine man, as you put it. I'm a lost man. You're mistaken. I'm not genuine. I'm a fantasy you cling to. There's nothing genuine there. The whole world is merely a game on a table for disappointed gamblers. You're playing—playing a game with me that I'm not good at."

"That's enough! Don't torment me anymore."

"You're just a dreamy girl. I should have spotted your game from the beginning. How can a girl like you rely on a vanquished man in shackles like me? By God, how naive I was! What a fool and idiot I was!"

"I love you. Why do you reject my love? You love me. I know that. But you want to be certain of your feelings. You're not entirely sure of yourself. You believe that my dream is bigger than you are. But, in spite of my youth, I'm nothing but a wretched girl. You're a lot for me. Let me look on you as a dream. Can we reject our dreams? Is that possible?"

"I'm confused. I feel that this is fairer than it should be—fair in an unfair world."

"Lovers don't set a price on their love. You love rivers and trees without expecting anything from them. True love makes no demands. We must give without accepting any payment. We must expect nothing at all in return."

"That's fairer than it should be."

"For a long time I dreamed of a man I had never seen, a man who couldn't offer any return for my love. Everything in this world can be bought and sold except for love. I don't want you to marry me, because marriage is a payment you would make to me. I love you the way you are—shackled, with nothing that I can hope to gain from you. For us to excel, we must set aside hope, that mirage for which we waste our whole life, wishing to obtain what it promises us—to no avail."

"Do you know—you're brilliant!"

"Like a heart that love has abandoned."

Light poured over the sole palm tree in the outer yard, making the dust-covered fronds glow. Meanwhile, a dove that had made her nest in the palm's canopy began to coo in a touching voice, as if chanting a musical refrain. This melody, however, was lost in the hubbub of the prisoners and the visitors, who created a ruckus that was hard on the ears.

Salwa laughed at this encounter, which was the seventh time I had met her, and asked, "Know what? A week ago I went on a school trip to a mountain."

"I love the mountains."

"It was a tall mountain near a river. I reached the summit the first time, although I stopped occasionally to catch my breath. A young man—one of my university friends—stayed beside me, urging me to climb ever higher. When I reached the peak, I saw all the plains and meadows spread out beneath my feet—green verging on blue. A mare was trotting at the valley's mouth. I spread my arms and yelled, 'I love the whole world! I love everything: butterflies, rocks, and caterpillars, everything in existence.'

"Then I heard, coming from the bottom of the mountain, music mixed with quavering voices and laughter that bubbled up from a deep reservoir, and the young man, my friend called to me, 'Come, come, you mountain goat.'"

"You shouldn't have returned."

"Then I descended the mountain and on the road asked myself whether I would love you again. I felt you might be dead by the time I visited you. But that was all just a fantasy I created for myself, because here you are standing beside me, smiling and playing the lover. Have you told Mun'im that we're in love? Don't. Let's deceive them a little. That won't hurt them. We've always been deceived about things,

things that happened behind our backs. Even so, my mother told me some days ago, 'I feel that Aziz is one of us.' What exactly did she mean? I don't know. It's not important that we know so long as we want nothing from them."

"I'm trembling."

"It's a fever, by God, the prophetic fever."

"I feel that I'm more alone than ever before."

"But you'll remain with us, united by defects and virtues."

"I'm trembling."

"It's a fever, by God, the prophetic fever. Advance, then, you visionary. Beyond the horizon lies a city with your name on it."

"I'm trembling. Leave me."

"Goodbye then."

The light on the solitary palm faded away while in my prophetic daze I traversed the rungs of a new wakefulness that I had never experienced before. People near me were conversing while I watched history collect inside a single flask and then pour forth over the world again—like anything else in this existence.

◻

During her final visit to the penitentiary I asked her, "Do you believe that a passing love like this can last?"

"I don't know. I frequently ask myself when I'm some place different or see a specific tree whether I'll return to see that place or that tree again before I die. But I always know that the place will continue to exist after me, and likewise the tree. Our love might not endure, but it can never die. It will continue linked to the air, the night, the trees, and the sap of life. Nothing dies. It survives as an image in the memory of existence."

"Oh, are we destined to persist in the memory of existence forever?"

"Exactly like that, without bodies. We will have turned into an idea."

"You're dreaming."

"I dream to contact my love."

"You'll bump into a wall there."

"I traverse walls. Have you forgotten that I'm an idea?"

"You can't resist all the way to the end."

"I'll try."

"What if you fail?"

"I'll find some other way."

"But, where to?"

"To nothingness, to the great void."

Eight

I had been awake for more than an hour but was still tossing around in my bed, oblivious to the boisterous voices that bounced off the walls. Although I wasn't really asleep, I wasn't really awake either. I felt I was pursuing an endless journey between sleep and wakefulness. From time to time I glimpsed a tree that stretched like a prodigious octopus in front of a river that flowed from a hill over which birds soared while lions crouched near the forest. I didn't feel any emotion, but this didn't prevent me from seeing that I was entering a new world I had never experienced before. Was I truly a stranger to this place I had never located on any terrestrial globe? I heard fish in schools splashing as they plunged forward. On the other side of the river I saw Salwa, who stood near a docile lion. I thought: He must have been her friend for a long time. The lion fled suddenly toward the far side of the valley while Salwa continued to giggle like a young girl at a school party.

"Where's Aziz? They want him."

I started suddenly, as if a horse had trod on my limbs. I rose and rubbed my scalp with my fingers. I heard Abdulkareem tell me, "They want you in the administration. Hurry up!"

"What do they want with me?"

"I don't know. They're waiting for you at the gate."

The truth was that I wanted to tarry longer in my dreams, to return to Salwa from whom the lion had fled to the far side of the valley. Even so, I consoled myself, "They must want me for some important reason. Perhaps they've decided to release me and throw me back on the street."

As he stood by the gate, the policeman asked me skeptically, "Are you Aziz Mahmud?"

Then, without waiting for my response, he jerked his head and commanded, "Let's go. They're waiting for you."

I proceeded through the iron gate and stood in the outer passage, watching the policeman lock the gate and head toward me. I walked along beside him, gazing at my shoes. I smiled to myself when I noticed that my right shoe was wobbling because its lace had come untied. I stood in front of the warden's office, waiting for the policeman, who had stepped in front of me and entered. He returned and pulled me inside with him. The warden was seated behind his desk while two men in civilian clothes sat on old sofas.

The warden cast me a disdainful glance before saying, "You stated in your petition on entering the penitentiary that you're not political and were arrested by mistake, but the reports reaching us tell a different story. You're not just an ordinary political activist, you're one of the extremists."

I said passionately, "That's a barefaced lie. They're lying to you."

63

I suddenly felt that the room's location had shifted. The policeman standing behind me had surprised me with a heavy blow to the back of my head, making me stagger. Then he began to yell at me, "When you stand before his Excellency the Warden, you must remain totally mute."

I regained my balance after almost falling and then asked the policeman, "Why did you hit me?"

One of the two seated men—a young fellow with an effeminate face—yelled, "Shut up, dog!"

The warden intervened, addressing me, "Did you think you could pull the wool over our eyes? Hundreds like you pass through here every day. It doesn't take us long to discover their true character, which they attempt to conceal behind an innocent, placid façade."

"But what have I done?"

The second man, who had remained silent until then, picked up a folder from the warden's desk, opened it, and—drawing a paper from it—said, "Since you entered prison, a number of reports about you have come in. Because you persist in proclaiming your innocence, I'll read you some of them.

"Report Number 1: 'Although Aziz Mahmud Sa'id clearly looks like an idiot, he's just as dangerous as the others. Since his arrival at the penitentiary he has attempted to strengthen his ties with revolutionary extremists like Mun'im, Husayn, and Salam. Likewise, he spends most of his time in discussions and in reading destructive books. He frequently listens attentively to political conversation and never stops his surveillance of those present. Although he tries to conceal his true nature, I believe he is a plant placed here to observe the prison's internal workings. After some time he will be released, since there is nothing with which to charge him.

Then he will present a report to his organization about each of the prisoners.'

"Report Number 2: 'I have imposed strict surveillance on him and believe that he is watching me too. He made fun of me once in front of the prisoners, saying, 'Justice has disappeared from this region of the world.' On another front, Aziz attempts to contact opponents of the prison committee with the goal of learning the true nature of the situation from the inside. He has been able to gain the trust of other inmates as he attempts to impose his hegemony over them. In one of the weekly meetings, he spoke for the first time and demonstrated clearly that he's not as stupid as he looks.'

"Report Number 3: 'Aziz Mahmud Sa'id did something this time that clearly revealed his identity. He supervised the production of a theatrical event in the prison. He took charge of writing the script and rehearsing with the actors.'"

The man stopped reading and glared at me, trying to gauge the impact that his reports had made on me. I thought: I've finally become really important. Like the others, I have crimes and offenses credited to me. But I also had my love, which shone like a dawn with millions of chirping birds. Here I stood before judges I didn't know while living among secretive spies who were trying to strip me of my cloak of innocence.

I heard the blustering warden bellow again, choppily, "Fine! Do you confess, now?"

"There's nothing for me to confess. I'm not affiliated with anyone."

"But the reports inculpate you."

"All it amounts to is that I'm living there with them."

"But that doesn't mean you should defend or protect them. They're the ones who told on you."

65

"Who?"

"Don't play the fool! You know who we mean. Do you want us to tell you their names?"

I didn't respond.

"Fine. If you're not one of them, prove it to us."

"How?" I asked. "I was arrested sitting in a café."

The young man with the effeminate face said, "We want you to work with us. If you demonstrate your sincerity, we'll release you eventually and return you to your job. If you wish, we can find you a better, higher-ranking post. You know we don't shortchange people who cooperate with us."

Attempting to remain calm, I said, "I was innocent before I entered the penitentiary. I wasn't the type of employee you suggest I should become."

The warden responded quietly, "Absolute innocence doesn't exist. Everything has its price."

"Do I have to become a spy in order to prove my innocence?"

My tone upset the young man with the effeminate face. He rose and walked toward me, gazing into my eyes as if he had received an unexpected insult from me. Then he said, "Get out, ass! Nothing works with you!"

As I left the room my buttocks received a powerful kick that propelled me outside. Then the policeman grabbed me by the right hand and dragged me back to the cell block. When I passed through the gate there, I felt queasy and racked with pain as the inmates gathered around me. The policeman insulted me contemptuously, "Get in there, coward!"

Then he turned to the inmates and, pretending to be their friend, cautioned, "Beware of him! He informed on you. They'll be calling some of you in for interrogation."

Stung by his words, I shouted, "He's lying! Lying!"

I anxiously walked a few steps forward, filled by a deep sense of wounded dignity. How could I counter an untruthful policeman's words? I saw sparks flying in the eyes that glared at me. They were condemning me, because only such a condemnation could justify their existence in the penitentiary. What myopia was this that so altered the color of things that brilliant day appeared darker than night? What madness was this that made a lie a palliative for consciences that suffered from invisible, mysterious burdens? What form of deliverance could be more vacuous than this, which a man achieved only by trampling on the dismembered body of his victim?

"He's lying! Lying!"

I noticed that Abdulkareem was standing at the front, gazing at me mockingly. I saw that the circle was beginning to widen around me, as if I were a clown at a village festival. It spread out, little by little, overstepping the boundaries of the small courtyard and the prison walls, encompassing the whole of Iraq, all of Asia, and then the world.

At first I saw dozens of eyes staring at me. I kept shouting dementedly, "He's lying! Lying!" Then they began to multiply exponentially, as if a plague had suddenly descended on the prison, generating new eyes at every moment. The eyes kept multiplying until I felt that they had become hundreds, thousands, no—millions. "He's lying! Lying!" My throat was parched, and the sun setting behind the walls had faded away, leaving nothing more than a washed-out shadow. Then the circle began to narrow, draw closer, and grow tighter, till I felt squeezed inside a bottle. I was trembling like a windswept tree while a thousand suns flashed overhead. Faces disappeared. Personal identities vanished. They drew closer to me as formless, gelatinous blobs. I heard myself breathing heavily.

So I told myself: This time you're in for a real drubbing. You should have been a magician so you'd know how to walk barefoot over fiery coals.

I found myself shouting loudly, "Leave me alone! How can you believe a policeman? I've not betrayed anyone!" Besieged, I felt I was climbing an endless ladder toward God. I dreamed I would die of pain. I awoke suddenly on feeling a lightning bolt blind my eye. Someone had struck my face.

I heard commingled cries:

"Beat him to death!"

"This is the spy!"

"A plant! Death to traitors!"

I heard their screams while writhing beneath their hysterical blows. I raised my hands to put them over my ears and attempted to shield my face with my elbows, folding in on myself. I didn't know how I could protect myself from their blows. Seized by an insane sense of yielding progressively to pain, I still did not stop thinking for a moment. I was amazed that a person could think beneath the weight of these blows, these hands that rose and fell chaotically, these rough feet that pulverized my submissive body. At that moment, Salwa dawned in my mind. She was huddled up, also receiving their kicks on her body, grasping my hand. Finally, however, she rose and stood before a frieze overlooking a bewildered night that spread over a white valley. A tumultuous crowd was ranged before her. I heard her yell at them, "Damn you!" They applauded her. Then I saw her smile again. Without any embarrassment, she stripped naked and lay down beneath me. I fell on her, torn by pain and desire. I was face down, and Salwa was there beneath me, between my thighs. I held her tight and she pressed me hard against her splendid body. Its fragrance so overwhelmed me that I dissolved into it, clinging to her hair. I was dying. They were kicking my head. Blood spread down over my face, filling my eyes. I heard Salwa moan too. Then I faded away, slipping into the night.

◻

Rays of sunshine came through a window in a room that smelled of naphthalene, while the wind shook the tree trunks in the garden. I tried to open my eyes, but a mysterious force prevented me. All the same, I resisted the pain that paralyzed my body. When I stretched my hand to my head I felt it blunder over a bandage soaked with iodine. Suddenly everything was clear to me—as if a brilliant light had fallen on a thicket of darkness where I had been wandering, lost. So I hadn't died. I was still able to think. I felt a kind of murky happiness mixed with rage. The wound was too deep for me to overlook. I thought about the enormous stupidity of those people who had wanted to slay me, without any genuine evidence, merely because a policeman had incited them against me. They had believed him without even listening to what I might say.

The bed where I lay was relatively comfortable. I felt pain in my left shoulder and realized that my left hand was fastened by a metal handcuff to the bed and held high, affecting the blood circulation.

Yes, I saw all those feet of stone falling on my face, leaving in my heart wounds that couldn't be bandaged. My God, why did they treat me so inhumanely? I had never consciously had a cause, but now I had acquired one I must defend, because this was the sole ordeal by which I could justify my existence. I had gained a cause the moment I was besieged like a fish flung on the sand. Hundreds of eyes had observed the festival of my death, whereas I had taken refuge in solitude as though the matter didn't concern me. One of my mistakes, which I was forced to acknowledge, was desiring to remain a loner without any tie to what the others were doing. For that reason, imagining that the matter did not concern me unless it directly harmed me, I had even kept quiet about the treachery of Abdulkareem, who had continued to submit his reports to the police. But now I had a cause, against my wishes. I wasn't afraid but sorrowful instead.

Soon the door opened and a nurse entered, followed by a policeman. The nurse said, "Great, you've finally come to."

Then he asked spontaneously, "Why did they do that to you? It's incredible."

Not wanting to discuss the matter with him, I replied, "I don't know."

The policeman commented sarcastically, "They never know anything."

The nurse said soothingly, "You almost died. What more can you ask for than recovery?"

I yelled in my pain, "Remove the handcuff at least. I can't bear that."

The policeman replied decisively, "No way! Orders prevent it. Do you want me to lose my job?"

"What orders? I'm dying from pain."

"Why don't you tell that to your comrades who beat you till you almost died?"

Then he added meanly, "Are you really a traitor as they alleged? What did you do?"

I kept silent, choking on my rage. I thought I would scream at him, but I knew he wouldn't tire of hurling insults at me.

The policeman turned to the nurse to tell him, "I need to close the window too. He might find some way to escape."

The smiling nurse replied, "Don't get carried away."

All the same the policeman proceeded to close the window and to pull down the shades. So the trees and sun disappeared from view.

The nurse laughed at him sarcastically, "You'd better keep a close eye on him. He may vaporize and escape through the cracks in the window."

"I know, I know," retorted the policeman. "I've devoted my whole life to serving them."

I wanted to cry but would have felt embarrassed. In fact I was ashamed of everything in the world and of everyone—policemen, nurses, and inmates. I turned my face to the wall, reflecting on the darkness that fills man's spirit. I heard the key turn in the lock. They had gone.

Then I felt free to weep without embarrassment.

◫

The next day I was summoned to appear before an interrogation committee. Panting behind a policemen, who led the way, I passed down the hall linking my room in the prison hospital to one of the rooms located at the building's end. He had removed my handcuffs but continued to carry them in his hand. I wondered: What do you suppose they're plotting for me this time? What do they want from me? I entered the room and stood motionless, staring at the faces. I had reached a decision that I wouldn't go easy on them anymore.

The interrogator seated in the middle stared at my face as well. Then I watched him open his mouth to say, "Fine. Tell us what you know."

I said, "I have nothing to say."

The man's annoyance showed on his face. He asked incredulously, "They beat you—isn't that so?"

I didn't respond.

"Tell us their names so we can interrogate them."

"I don't know any of them."

The man appeared to disapprove of my position. "But you certainly know the reason."

"There wasn't any reason."

The man seated beside the interrogator exploded, looking up from the papers he had been busily reading all this time. "Don't be a numbskull. They themselves accuse you of working with us."

Ignoring his attempt to incite me against the other inmates, I said, "I don't work with anyone."

The man continued his provocation, "But your comrades believe that you submitted reports on them."

I said sarcastically, "You know the truth of that better than they do."

The third man, previously silent, intervened, "So what? Do you believe that working with us for the welfare of the nation would be a disgrace? Your position suggests that you're against the system. If you're really sincere, you won't hesitate to provide any information that would root out the nation's saboteurs. We ourselves work for the system. Do you consider our work disgraceful?"

Trying to escape the trap the man was preparing for me, I commented, "Each man has the work he chooses for himself."

The man sitting in the middle replied, "It's clear that you hate us—and yet you claim to be innocent."

I asked calmly, "Must I love you for you to consider me innocent?"

Suddenly the man who had talked about disgrace rose and slapped my face, which was wrapped in bandages. I felt the room evaporate before my eyes as I fell into darkness. Even so, I struggled to keep from falling. I wanted to remain on my feet at any cost. A trickle of blood descended from my brow, reached the edge of my right eyebrow, trailed down my nose to its tip, and reached my lips. I stuck out my tongue and tasted it. It was salty and tainted with iodine. The man who had hit me returned to his place, cursing me with words I didn't grasp. Then I heard the man in the middle say, "We'll send you back to your comrades to tear you to pieces. That's the best punishment for you."

Sensing blood fill my mouth and darkness envelope my eyes, I found myself spitting in his face, as if I was spitting in the face of all my personal dilemmas. I was plunged into a night where I was searching for a sun beyond the horizon, beyond a breaker whipped high by the wind.

Nine

They didn't send me back to my cell block, because everything had changed. I had suddenly become a matter of urgent concern to them after months as nothing more than a forgotten number on a roster, ignored by everyone. Now that I had spat in their interrogator's face, I was more than a forgotten number.

I remember only obscurely what happened to me next, or at least some of it. One of them seized me by my hair and struck my face while another kicked my butt. I decided not to scream no matter what it cost me, since the idea of screaming embarrassed me. But it wasn't easy, because I fell on my back and the man whose face I had targeted sat on my chest and started beating me between the eyes. I vainly tried to stop him. I remember that they were cursing me. Along with their curses I heard a love song from a radio playing in another room.

I thought I had embroiled myself in more trouble than I should have. I wondered how I should have reacted—as I did?

Should I have insulted them the way I did? Yes, I think so. Despite all my misery, happiness overwhelmed me—a happiness of self-satisfaction. At times it's necessary for a person to sacrifice even his life for the sake of something that seems very ordinary or even invisible, although it sheds light on our situation in life. I thought I would fight. But for whom? I wouldn't fight like Salam, who found meaning for his struggle in bossing the others around. I wouldn't fight like Mun'im, who projected himself into the future. I fought for my own sake. Didn't I have a right to fight on my own behalf? Didn't I—like the others—have a right to my own personal wars? In this war of mine, I received their blows and blood flowed from my nose. I felt I was stronger than all of them, stronger than all the statesmen, policemen, and inmates.

The policeman standing outside the room entered and grabbed my hair, beating me with his wire-wrapped stick. One of the interrogators told him, "Drag this dog away. We'll know how to tame him!"

The policeman, who hadn't stopped striking me, said, "I'll make you wish you were dead."

The three interrogators were panting from exhaustion. Despite everything, I was very happy—happier than at any time in the past. I had challenged my fear and accepted the destiny I had chosen for myself. I collapsed on the floor outside the office, so the policeman kicked my belly. "Get up, wretch!"

I heard one of the interrogators say, "He belongs in Penitentiary 3. I'll telephone them."

I rose as blood from my nose stained my pajama top. Hearing what the interrogator had said, the policeman commented menacingly, "There you'll kiss their hands to stop them from beating you. Have you ever been in the torture chamber?"

I was silent. I felt he was amused by the thought of the torture I would receive there. Perhaps he wanted me to kiss his hands too. I stood—as though confronting a beast that had come to attack me—and walked forward, as I always did, as if heading to the party of my life.

◫

On the way to Penitentiary 3, I saw the city for the first time in months. I was truly dazzled by the buildings that glittered in the sunlight and the trees that released heady fragrances. Youths, young women, and tribal Arabs were strolling along nonchalantly. Three children, however, stopped and applauded, laughing. I was unclear about the true nature of their sentiments. Perhaps they were applauding me as an imprisoned hero to encourage me to be resolute. Or perhaps the applause was for the policemen between whom I sat in the open military vehicle. I tried to wave to them, but my hands were shackled. So I merely raised them over my head. I was surprised that the two policemen allowed me this provocative gesture. I brought my hands close to my left pocket and with the fingers of my right hand extracted my pack of cigarettes. Then I brought both hands near my mouth and plucked one out. I didn't want to offer a cigarette to the policemen but they held out their hands and took some from the pack. I didn't protest. They thanked me. Then one of them—an old man with a farmer's face— turned toward me, asking, "What did you do before you were arrested?"

I felt like tormenting him. "I'm an engineer."

The younger policeman turned toward me respectfully and said, "You must have earned a large salary."

I continued to lie: "Oh, not too large—only a hundred dinars."

The old man responded incredulously, "A hundred dinars! That's more than I make in an entire year."

Then he asked, "Are you married?"

"No."

Shaking his head, he commented, "If you were married, you wouldn't have gotten involved in politics. When you marry, you'll think a thousand times before setting foot in prison again."

◨

I stood before one of the clerks in Penitentiary 3, clasping my hands behind my back, my head slanted toward my left shoulder, not knowing whether I should speak or not. The two policemen, who had removed the chain from my wrists, were standing behind me. One of them said, "Record his name and call someone to receive him."

The clerk raised his head to look at me while I listened to the clamor of passersby. He was an old man with gray hair and a mustache that drooped over the corners of his mouth. I stared back at him. Confronted by all the papers that covered his desk, he looked tired to me.

He asked the two policemen, "Where are his papers?"

The young policeman answered, "He has no papers. The warden told us he would spend a few days with you before returning."

The clerk flared up and said in a loud voice, "I don't care what the reason is. He must have his own set of papers."

"We were told to bring him to this facility, and that's what we've done."

The clerk nervously tossed the papers lying in front of him on the ground and said, "I can't accept responsibility for his presence here without the official papers."

The elderly policeman begged, "But what are we supposed to do?"

The clerk answered, "Take him away. I can't accept him."

"What a mess this is!"

The young policeman cast an angry glance at me, as if I were responsible for his predicament. Then he stretched out his hand and grabbed my wrist. "Come. Let's see the duty officer."

He rapped on the door and I followed him in while the other policeman remained outside. He saluted the duty officer in a way that seemed ridiculous to me. The officer raised his head to ask, "What do you want?"

The youthful policeman replied in a rhetorical vein, "They have sent this detainee with us from Cell Block 5, but the clerk refuses to admit him, because he's not accompanied by papers."

The officer glanced back at the papers spread across his desk. Lifting a slip of paper in his fingers, he asked, "Are you Aziz Mahmud Sa'id?"

Astonished, I said, "Yes, I am."

The officer nodded his head, "Woe to you! We'll make you curse the day you were born. How did you dare strike the interrogator? Are you mentally deranged or do you want to challenge us?"

I responded hopelessly, "I didn't strike anyone."

The policeman suddenly cut me off. "Shut up, ass! Don't you see that you're speaking to an officer?"

The officer laughed sarcastically and looked at me encouragingly, "Why don't you hit him too? He's insulted you."

78

I didn't think of hitting him. The situation seemed dangerous to me despite the officer's encouraging smiles. Then, addressing the policeman, he said, "Tell the clerk that our guest is an exceptional fellow who carries no papers. They telephoned me to accept him for a stay of a few days in our hotel till we teach him how to behave."

He smiled as he spoke to me. When I smiled too at his comic manner of speaking, he suddenly roared at me, "Get out of my face! I'll see a lot of you!"

◫

In the cell, where I lay on the bare floor, there were two other men lost in their own thoughts, each crouched in a corner of the small room. The first of them, a young man of about twenty-five, spent the whole night propped against the wall, leaning his head on his contracted knees. I didn't know whether he was asleep or not, since he never raised his head. I wondered what this barefooted youth was thinking about. He had been brutally tortured without uttering a word. From my room I heard the frenzy of the torturers and the whine of their whips. But the victim remained mute until the end. I thought: his silence must distress them. Screaming is merely a trap to which the torturer attempts to lure his victim. Silence, however, frightens most torturers profoundly.

"Beat him! Strike!"

"Say something! Confess!"

"You won't escape in one piece from us."

I felt their whips scorch my skin too, even though I was sitting in the bare room, awaiting my turn. Could I remain silent too? My torturer would be delighted if I knelt and howled like a dog. No, I would have to relinquish control over every part of my body in order to remain silent, not to protect any secret from them but to free my heart from fear.

"Oh, I'm exhausted. He won't confess."

"He can't remain firm till the very end."

Hearing the voices of the torturers, I shuddered in spite of myself. My God, what was this pleasure the torturer derived from inhumane treatment of a defenseless person?

"Go on: tie his shoulders to the fan."

He must be strung up now between the torturers, who were panting from fatigue. I heard one of them say, "Let him swing. Hit him. Strike!"

I could visualize him swinging there between them, strung up by his shoulders, which were tied from behind, while sticks and rubber hoses wrapped with wire sank into his flesh. He swung silently, as though the matter concerned someone else.

"That's enough. I need a smoke."

"He's a hero. I love the heroes."

"That's fine. Be resolute, hero. But for how long?"

The torturer wasn't kidding. He meant what he said. The torturers hate weak victims, because they see themselves in them. The strong ones provide them with an occupational delight that gives meaning to their lives.

I asked myself: Do you suppose these torturers tell stories about their victims to their wives and friends? Perhaps even to their children? They must. I believe man can pervert things even without a pretext. This is the case with the torturer who lives off contempt for human dignity.

"Snuff out your cigarette on his body!"

"Ha, aren't you afraid of fire, hero?"

"I'll burn his lips so he remembers us when he kisses his wife."

"Be strong, hero! Be strong!"

I smelled burning flesh from the other room. It reminded me of the scent of spring weeds. I wondered whether a man might prefer death to life at times. I didn't really know, but man doesn't feel that way until life becomes impossible unless accompanied by a total acceptance of death.

The other man, a worker in his forties, had been struck in the arm by a bullet that had not yet been removed. He was hit in a demonstration that swept down al-Rasheed Street. He was bleeding and moaned continuously, cursing everyone. I didn't know why they had left him like that, without treatment. Perhaps his face was so odious that they wanted him to die. Pricks of conscience about him made me feel terrible—as if I were responsible for his wound. He was weeping. At first I felt sorry for him, but I also hated him because I was unable to do anything for him. I was ignored too, in my corner of the cell, waiting for my turn on the torturers' docket.

The closed door finally opened and two people whose faces I couldn't make out in the faint light headed toward me. As usual it was late. Torturers prefer to work after midnight. I saw one of them gesture toward me as if inviting me to a party, "Come, stand up. We're waiting for you most eagerly."

As I left the door of my cell, heading for the torture chamber, I decided to relinquish my claims to my body, which they envied, since it was my true prison within the prison. I shone like a city in the sunlight.

Ten

When I awoke I found myself stretched out on a comfortable bed in Salam's room. I was surrounded by many smiling faces. These were the same faces that had angrily encircled me while shoes battered my head. I was disconcerted and didn't know what to do or say. I found myself in an awkward situation—like being surprised having sex. Should I curse them? If not, what should I do? They had cruelly disgraced me, placing a crown of thorns on my head, when they should have been receiving me like a brother in their family. I wondered whether I should disappoint them—these sympathetic wretches. I wasn't able to love them after what they had done to me. They were smiling at me. Should I smile too? I wanted to weep, but should I weep in front of these men? I felt incapable of doing anything. All the same, when Salam stretched out his hand, placing it on my head, I felt fraternal affection for all of them. I was with them once more. Despite everything, they were as innocent as I was. The gist of the matter was that the victim's role is not fulfilled until he becomes a torturer, whether by the law of chance or some fantasy of dogma.

Salam said affectionately, "We committed an atrocious mistake with you. I hope you'll forget what happened."

I smiled, "It seems that mistakes are always inevitable."

"The policeman lied to us and incited the inmates against you. In any case, we discovered the true traitor."

I said calmly, "I knew his identity from the start."

Salam seemed shocked, "Did you know? Why didn't you tell us then?"

"I didn't want to take sides in a matter concerning you. It was Abdulkareem. One rainy evening I saw him passing reports to the night guard."

An inmate commented, "It's unfortunate we didn't learn the truth till after he was released."

I said, laughing, "I've learned to distrust obese men."

Salam said with embarrassment, "That won't happen again. I've suffered a lot."

When I tried to sit up, my head fell on the pillow. I turned to one side and wept silently, feeling my innocence slide from my numb fingers, which rested on my knee. I no longer heard their voices, which were as faint as leaves falling in the forest. In the profound calm permeating my heart, I searched for Mun'im's face and heard Salwa's voice calling me. I assumed that the sound was inspired by a fantasy or by love. A wave approached the shore. It was topped by froth like an anthem sung by a mixed choir of a thousand. Then it collided with white boulders, which stretched as far as the eye could see, before receding as if night had fallen over everything.

Here—enveloped in clouds—was Salwa, dawning once more from obscurity. My God, why does she always emerge this way in my memory like the morning star when cares besiege me? Always Salwa. Salwa the eternal fantasy. But now Salwa had suddenly disappeared from my life too—like everything else. How fantastic my belief had been that Salwa might be mine! I know I've misled myself a lot and perhaps have invented realities that don't exist, hearing words she didn't utter. Perhaps Salwa never existed. She might have been a fantasy borne by my spirit and then attached to a pine tree I saw in a beatific vision across the meadows, gleaming from afar like a butterfly in a stream of light. By night, between two ancient blankets, I would feel her cotton thighs and twist right and left, feeling embarrassed that eyes might have been studying me.

Salwa vanished suddenly. She stopped writing and stopped visiting too. I felt she had renounced all of us. I was upset and confronted this truth that arrived when I was unprepared to receive it. I had known from the beginning, although I had not possessed enough courage to face up to myself, that a love like this was doomed. So what had she wanted from me? Was I merely a temporary pawn in her game? A game with a comic ending? No. No, that was impossible, because she was too beautiful and too just for that. Perhaps she had wished to open a door to love for me, as if she were saying, "Always look ahead. All you need is a path." But I needed something more than a path—the courage to overstep my shackles, both within my spirit and outside of it.

I asked Mun'im once, a few days before they released him, when I felt totally frustrated, "Why has Salwa stopped visiting us?"

He replied sarcastically, "Perhaps she's found people who deserve her love more than we do."

"But . . . ."

"Why? Don't you know she believes in free love, which should be equitably distributed to all of mankind?"

⊡

At the time, I felt that my life had stopped at a depot that had never been my destination. All the old dreams that had filled my head concerning the world suddenly dissipated. I wondered how the prison experience was able to turn everything I had previously learned about the world upside down. In any case, I was no longer that harebrained fellow who had believed the world couldn't be happy unless he was, perhaps because I had wanted to fashion everyone to my pattern. But all that has ended now, thank God. Did I have to say, "All that has ended"? I didn't know. But something in my heart kept telling me that the moment we think something has ended, that thing has just begun. What came before was merely a zero. Could I say then that I had lived the previous years as a zero?

I stretched my hand out to my mother's letter that had arrived a few days earlier and stared at its green ink. I didn't intend to read it. I had read it once and become even sadder. I may well have hated the letter, which was stuffed full of sentiments injurious to a man like me, who was no longer the person he used to be. I sensed that Mustafa, the old man who looked like an anarchist with long tresses, the village

85

prophet who had been sentenced to death two weeks earlier and who would be executed in a few hours, was closer to me than this letter, which discussed an attorney who would work to achieve my release. None of that meant anything to me in comparison to the death that would carry Mustafa away at dawn. I thought that Mustafa was certainly not sleeping. Like me he must be thinking now, in his cell in an adjoining block behind the cell block where I lived. I remembered how he had sat with us in the right-hand corner of the wall opposite me, beneath the electric light near the prison's radio, alone and silent like a Buddhist monk in his temple. Then he would suddenly explode, releasing a cry or scream of wonderment at some event, only to return once more to his profound silence. I wondered what he was thinking about now. At that time I felt he was with me. His destiny weighed on my heart. I could sense him now, that silent, problematic person who was leaving the world, awaiting his death, more alive than all the rest of us: than me, the mercurial person who carried his corpse around on his shoulders; than Salam announcing intemperate, revolutionary class warfare like a dream in the most remote future; than Abdulkareem the secret agent who played the role of a combatant only to leave; than Salwa who had wounded my heart; and than Mun'im who had packed his head with thoughts about another, new world.

The guard standing on the wall that surrounded the cell block called out as loudly as he could, "They're preparing the gallows now."

Then he added, "A fine man, but it's said many died because of him. May God be with him in his ordeal."

I asked the guard, "What do you suppose Mustafa's doing now?"

The guard could see the prison's other courtyard, where the gallows was being prepared. "I don't know, but he's a man. He must face his death courageously."

"Would you retain your courage if you were the man being hanged?"

He guffawed loudly at the thought and added, "I believe I'd shit in my pants. The world would be a despicable place if I didn't have a wife and children."

Then he asked me, as if seeking my agreement, "How about you? Would you shit in your pants too?"

I felt a deep desire to remain silent. All the same I told him noncommittally, "I don't know. Nothing seems important anymore."

I set off, walking away from him, but heard him remark, "You ought to get married. Then you'd know how hard or painful it is when a man is imprisoned or hanged."

◘

Hard and painful? Did those terms suffice to describe what I felt about a man who was condemned to be hanged in a few hours? Perhaps each of us felt a pain peculiar to himself, but Mustafa's pain was something only he knew. Unlike me, he wouldn't live to narrate the suffering of a man who has been strung up by a rope expertly twisted around his neck. I hadn't had the opportunity to witness a man being hanged according to the special protocol they were following now, but when I was a child I saw something similar. Thousands of people had gone out into the streets in bloody, angry demonstrations, holding colored banners aloft. Footsteps were swift and screams shrill. I remember that everyone was yelling like crazy. A man with a dark complexion fired a number of shots from his revolver at a locked store. Then others began using stones and sticks to break neon lights, shop windows, and the signs of stores and taverns. I was really living through a weird type of carnival. Men had always seemed sage and stalwart to me, not excited by thrilling games. At this time, they appeared to be children like us, engrossed in a game to its end. I felt I was one of them and that we had to vanquish our temporary enemies, whose existence was presupposed by the rules of the game, the way we always played.

When I was eight or nine, the neighborhood children would gather in front of the door of a rich man's house and choose a commander and a flag for our army. I was always a foot soldier. I stood and listened to our commander, who would order us to seize the bases of children from nearby neighborhoods, rip down their flags and rub them in the mud. Our weapons were sticks and stones, although some of the older children armed themselves with knives stolen from their homes. Once, when we attacked an enemy area, our army was defeated. Our commander was captured then, beaten, and held prisoner. Instead of surrendering, however, he drew his knife and stabbed an older child his age. I was terrified and fled back to our base in front of the house of the wealthiest man in our community, feeling that something momentous had happened, although it overwhelmed me.

Now I was overwhelmed once more as I watched these men attack each other. I would need to pick a team, so I chose to side with the victorious army. I didn't know the defeated men, but they certainly were our enemies. I hurried along with the overflowing human wave that was surging forward. Feet moved out of cadence and yells emerged from deep inside throats on that amazing evening. I heard a man scream at us, "Attack! Smash everything!"

Many had rushed into shops encountered on their way after breaking down the locked doors. They proceeded to carry off everything they could lay hands on. I saw two men who were transporting a television set while shouting slogans in the name of the masses. A man stood in front of a shop yelling, "Stop! What are you doing? We're not thieves."

A farm worker retorted, "They're our enemies. Go get your share too. Don't be a puritanical Hanbali."

The man protested, "No way! I can't. What a disgrace!"

He hesitated, uncertain whether he was wrong or not. Then he looked around with embarrassment. When he was sure that no one was paying any attention to him, he entered the looted store too, shouting slogans in the name of the people.

Someone grabbed me by the hand, scolding me. "What are you doing here? Go back home, little boy, before a stray bullet hits you."

I didn't return home. I went with the people until I reached the square called al-Maydan, where thousands of people were clamoring with sporadic screams. From a distance of only meters, I saw a young man being beaten. His face was smeared with blood. I heard him scream, pleading with a middle-aged man, "I beg you. Save me. I swear I'm not one of them."

The man, however, kicked him so forcefully that he fell on his face on the asphalt. Then the man stepped forward and pounded the young man's face with his shoe. "I know exactly who you are, dog. We'll string you up with the others."

On the far side of the street, two naked corpses dangled from utility poles as mirthful people danced around them. A few men grabbed the bloodied youth and dragged him to a nearby post, which a man with bulging muscles climbed. The youth was wailing, since he saw the fate awaiting him. Despite the blood that coated his face and eyes, I could see tear drops glisten on his red cheeks. The muscular man drew the end of a rope up and passed it over one of the protruding bars before lowering it down to the bystanders, who placed a noose around the neck of the bloodied youth. A number of men shot off, pulling on the end of the rope. The young man was screaming, "I beg you. I kiss your hands. I haven't done anything to harm you."

Suddenly I saw his eyes bulge out and heard his voice choke as his feet were lifted off the ground. He continued to kick like a madman. He rose half a meter off the ground and continued to struggle against his death, staring directly into my eyes. The masses congregated in the square erupted in applause. The body finally went rigid and remained suspended in the void after the men tied the rope, fastening it to a utility pole. Then they stood gazing admiringly at the victim they had created.

I saw on the sidewalk opposite me three children who were throwing stones at the corpses, so I went to join their game. Pointing at a suspended corpse, one of them asked me, "Can you hit his prick?"

The hanged man was totally naked and his penis was dangling slackly between his hairy thighs. I said, "I'll try."

But when I cast my stone, I struck his open mouth. The children laughed and one told me, "You broke his teeth. . . . He won't be able to chew his food anymore."

□

On the other side of the penitentiary, Mustafa was saying goodbye to the world, perhaps with a sorrow blended with his elemental understanding of heroism. If I had been sitting in his cell at that time, I wouldn't have slept for a single moment—not out of fear but for the sake of life, which must be lived to the fullest until the final moment. Life's harshness does not cancel out the truth that it is the most beautiful thing in existence—more beautiful and profound than anything else. I asked myself: Do you suppose it's possible for a person to die before despair takes control of him? Certainly not. I don't believe so. A man struggles against death's infection until the last gasp. But this harshness, which death lays bare, does not justify even a single moment of treachery. For that reason, life must be lived honorably. When death brings honor to life, we must accept it calmly and silently so we don't betray the memory of our existence in the world, no matter what the circumstances.

It was about four in the morning and I was leaning against a prison wall, seated on a concrete bench, staring at the night that filled the sky as spring breezes carried to my nostrils the mixed scents of the many flowers outside. All the other prisoners had retreated to their rooms and fallen asleep. They had grieved sincerely for Mustafa's death, but had left it at that. What could they do? I thought, however: I can't sleep and leave him alone. If I'm unable to assist him in any way, at least I'll stay awake with him on his final night. It's true that a wall separates us, that he's locked in a cell wearing red garments, and that the gallows has been set up, but I feel it would be disgraceful for me to fall asleep or to desert him, to allow him to face death alone. My conscience was adamant in not allowing me to betray him even for a single moment.

What about the other men's consciences? Yes, each of them had a conscience. But they wanted it to be a beneficial conscience, a conscience that permitted them to sleep and to dream of their wives, even when a dear friend was executed only meters from them.

That night I smoked an entire pack of cigarettes. The last one was in my fingers when I heard through the wall voices of men talking in the other courtyard and a hammer driving in nails. I thought that the executioners must have awakened. Here they were adding their finishing touches to the gallows that must bear the weight of a man suspended by his neck.

"Be absolutely sure of the beams' strength!"

That must be the warden. The monotonous pounding on wood increased. My whole body was shaking. I tried to control my knees but failed. I was afflicted by a fever in my nervous system. I saw before me a desert that stretched to the horizon. I was searching for something in it, perhaps for Mustafa's preposterous life, perhaps for Salwa, who no longer wrote to me. I felt very thirsty but had no desire to drink any water, whether from sorrow or shame on confronting death. Oh— why didn't Salwa write me anymore? Why was everything this way? Why?

Eleven

ore months passed without my being released from prison. I was no longer upset the way I had been at the beginning, on first arriving in Cell Block 5. I had grown so accustomed to life here I had forgotten what the other life in the streets was like, perhaps due to my new conviction that guilt is hardly a relevant consideration when a person is placed in prison. What it boils down to is that he enters prison one way or another. It's up to him to adjust to the destiny allotted to him. All the same, I never lost the feeling that the world outside also possessed its own special temptations. When one of my friends was released, I occasionally experienced a pang that quickly subsided, not because I envied him but because I had lost him. For this reason, with time, I trained myself to avoid forging strong ties to other prisoners. The same thing happens in wars. Whether in a war or a prison, we shouldn't love anyone too much because we may lose them at any moment, although the ways of parting differ.

About a month earlier I had been advised to submit a request that I be released, or at least charged, but nothing had happened. Then I learned from a sergeant in the penitentiary that my presence there without a file or an indictment had begun to make the administration nervous. For a long time they had postponed reviewing my status to avoid involving themselves in a case as dubious as mine, because how could I have been arrested unless I had my own file? What the sergeant told me was not mere conjecture. A few days later I was summoned to the office of the penitentiary's police supervisor. Smiling, he instructed me, "Sit down and let's search for a solution to your problem. A man without a file? How have we held you all this long time?"

I replied jovially, "You should have thrown me out, but you haven't."

"Rubbish! It's not that simple."

"Is it my fault that you've lost my file?"

"Lost your file? Who said that? You simply have never had a file. Under these circumstances your presence could arouse suspicions about you. Perhaps you have taken the place of an escaped prisoner whose absence has gone undetected at roll call."

"But that's absurd, as you know."

"Fine! Let's think of a way for you to emerge from your dilemma."

Then, noticing that I was still standing, he added, "Come on. Sit down. Why are you standing like that?"

I sat on a chair to the left of his wooden desk, on which many files and papers were stacked. He offered me a cigarette, which I accepted without thanks. I said, "Fine. What's to be done?"

Gazing at me, he replied, "We've written to all the police and security agencies to find out about you but have received no information. No one knows anything about you. We likewise do not know why you were arrested. Why were you?"

"I've already told you, but you didn't believe me. I was arrested by mistake, for no reason at all. I was sitting in a café when they took me to a detention facility where I spent a few days before I was transferred here. I hope that what I say will provide you with adequate grounds for releasing me now, at least."

The police supervisor laughed, saying, "It's not as simple as you believe. Unless a charge is brought against you, you will remain our guest forever. No one would believe you. The police don't arrest people from cafés for no reason at all. You must provide us with some plausible explanation for your arrest."

"Those are the facts. What more do you want?"

He replied somewhat conspiratorially, "The government's currently reviewing the inmates' files. A committee is looking at the prisoners' cases and will certainly inquire about you. Your affair will raise doubts when they learn that you have been incarcerated without a file. For that reason we must present a reasonable justification for your stay in the penitentiary for all this time. Everything must be logical. The cause of chaos everywhere is the lack of logic, without which everything falls apart. Every law enforcement officer in the world learns this principle."

Then he added, "What would you think about our devising a minor crime for you—some time in the past? Then we'll quickly release you. That would make everything much simpler for you and for us."

I surreptitiously tossed my cigarette butt on the floor and rubbed it out with my foot before I replied in a similarly jocular manner, "Fine. What crime do you want me to commit?"

The police supervisor, who had a puffy face, was concentrating in a way that looked ridiculous to me, and his expression was as blank as a hunk of metal. He replied, "I recommend a political offense so we can explain why you were in our penitentiary."

Playing along with him, I asked, "What do you suggest, for example?"

He answered, "What would you think, for example, of cursing the head of state in a café before a crowd of people? We'll persuade the café's owner and waiter, along with some policemen, to testify against you."

I said disapprovingly, "No, no, I don't want that. It's a serious charge."

Laughing, he replied, "It's not at all serious. It won't get you more than six months, whereas you've already spent more than twenty months in the penitentiary. So . . . what do you say?"

"Find me a crime that has no bearing on the head of state."

He thought a little before asking, "What would you think about striking a policeman on the street?"

"Why would I hit him?"

"Because you hate the police."

"No," I said. "Contrive a reasonable, logical crime for me, since the reason for the sorry state of things in the world is a lack of logic, as you pointed out."

He responded most earnestly, "It's a symbolic crime to simplify your release. Don't make things difficult for us."

When he found I wasn't eager to commit the crimes he was suggesting, he said, as though tired of thinking, "Since we still have a few more days, I'll think up a beautiful offense for you. You can count on me."

I thanked him for his concern and returned to my room in Cell Block 5, accompanied by a policeman who had been standing by the police supervisor's door, listening to our conversation. On the way back, he told me, "The police supervisor's a fine man. He'll arrange everything for you. Don't worry. He's in a pickle too. But he'll discover an appropriate solution. We don't usually encounter problems like this. A few months ago, when I was transporting nine undocumented aliens to the border, one managed to escape by profiting from the moment when they were being transferred from one vehicle to another. I wouldn't have been much concerned about his fate had I not been responsible for delivering nine—not eight—individuals. My fellow policemen were so worried they couldn't think straight. But I quickly hit upon a solution. I asked them to wait just a few minutes. Then I set off down the street to search for a replacement. At first I encountered some difficulty. I was guided to a solution when I saw a row of bootblacks who were sitting on the curb. I stood in front of them, needing to choose one. I offered my shoes to an adult, commenting, 'You must live alone here.' He replied, 'Certainly not. I have a large family and must provide food for my children. We all support our families.' A youth sitting beside him laughed and said, 'Except me.' I asked him, 'Don't you have a family?' He replied, 'They've all died, sir.'

"When the mature bootblack finished shining my shoes, I asked the youngster, 'What's your name?' He answered, 'Jum'a.' I told him in a reassuring tone, 'Come along, Jum'a. Come with me.' He asked me, 'But why?' I was forced to lie and told him, 'There's better work for you than shining shoes.' I made him think that a golden opportunity awaited him. He wanted to bring his box with him, but I told him, 'Leave that here. You won't be gone long.' But he never returned. Jum'a filled the vacancy left by the cursed man who had fled from us. I was truly touched by Jum'a's case, but he was a suitable replacement. If I had taken the older man, my conscience would have tormented me. I had a right to do that, because I didn't want to get fired just because a worthless, undocumented alien had escaped from our custody."

⊡

More than a month passed, but the police supervisor didn't call me back to discuss the invention of an appropriate crime. It seemed that he had found some solution all by himself, discovering his own special fix. I didn't pay much attention to the matter because I had grown resigned, perhaps because I felt at ease in the penitentiary, even though I had lost my freedom. I began to wonder what I would do if they cast me outside the prison's walls. I had lost my job and wouldn't be able to obtain any other employment. It pained me to be a rootless person, since there was no one I could rely on. Oh, what a fool I had been to believe that Salwa could be the cause that justified my return to the world from which I had been banished. She had been nothing more than one of the daydreams that stormed through my head whenever I was alone. Everything had changed. Now I found my freedom and happiness in this miserable abode that demanded nothing from me—where friends, cigarettes, food, and books were all free of charge too. What more than that did I want from the world?

All the same, I couldn't prevent myself from looking beyond myself. I kept dreaming of an apartment overlooking the Tigris River and of a girl on whom I spied through a crack in the door. The dream was repeated every night but with different details, as if it were a single story with a thousand scenarios. When I woke from my dream I would smoke a cigarette as I gazed around the room at my comrades who slept cheek by jowl—both friends and strangers at the same time—telling myself: What marvelous friends we are! Here we bed down together the way we did millions of years ago inside caves near the dinosaurs' boulder.

I felt the seasons slip past me in succession, as oblivious to me as if I were inert. In order to remain objective about my limited understanding, I would always ask myself: What precisely do I want from the world? I believe I no longer know where truth lies hidden and whether the surprises that the world unleashes on us in the form of waves of memories, living accommodations, and dreams also function as seasons in the lengthy, human game. Aside from that, this day seemed magical, since it appeared to me to be even more radiant than all the others that had swept over me without leaving any trace in my heart or memory.

Here the cold winter sun was illuminating the tops of the walls, gradually descending halfway down, splitting the yard into two sections: a long tract in the sun and another shaded one. Near the wall were human groupings—four if I included myself. Three young men were sitting on the left, all of them approximately the same age—between eighteen and twenty. They wore dark pajamas. The one on the left wore a red cap with a white band around it. They were discussing—in a regretful tone—sexual relations with the girls they knew.

Near them, sparrows pecked at empty food dishes strewn on the ground, gleaning scattered grains of rice. Propping an elbow against a wall of the coffeehouse room, an old man was drinking tea with a teacher from one of the southern villages. To my right stood two Kurds, who spoke of mountains coated with snow in winter as if these were legendary abandoned fortresses and about bears that abduct village maidens to take as their wives.

◻

Life in the cell block changed somewhat because the penitentiary's administration transferred a large number of inmates to different locations and also released others. Some men went to distant prisons after courts-martial had pronounced despotic sentences upon them. But the penitentiary was never empty. There were always new prisoners coming to us in successive waves. Thus, after two years of incarceration, I became one of the old-timers. Salam had been sentenced to ten years. So we hugged him goodbye with tears in our eyes. Rafi' was transferred with other inmates to banishment facilities located in the heart of the desert. After the inmates of Cell Block 5 were gradually dispersed every which way, only inmates in transit—most of them grumbling students who felt oppressed by the prison's high walls—remained. I derived a lot of enjoyment from talking to them and encouraging them. Life in the penitentiary had changed without any major upheaval. My friends left without me feeling this was a calamity, and in time I forged new friendships with the new arrivals. Salman the railway worker returned to his wife. After being fired, he abandoned the trains he had once ridden by night. Perhaps he was now working as a waiter in a restaurant, a driver, or anything else that occurred to him. Husayn, the village teacher, had also been released, returning to his profession but to a school far from his previous village. He had written me to say, "It's difficult for a person to bear the weight of his own existence in this paltry world."

I no longer felt tied to a society that appeared to me to be more like a corpse than anything else. The only people for whom I felt any affection now were the victims, the men with whom I lived in the penitentiary. I felt they were my brothers, because they existed on the world's other side, along with the destructive agitators.

Mun'im visited me only once—to tell me that Salwa was engaged and would soon be married. I realized that Salwa was a woman reserved for another world—people for whose sake the sun rises each morning—whereas I was merely one of those who exhaust themselves in a procession that stops at no station. I didn't feel any pain at losing her, because I knew I always lost anything I obtained. In a certain sense I was happy for her sake, since she would have found nothing in my heart but a lethal microbe she wouldn't have had the strength to withstand. It appeared to me that Mun'im had changed a lot. It seemed to me that he had died. I surprised him by asking, "What's happened to you? You're no longer the man I knew."

He replied agitatedly, "All books are fallacious and misleading. I no longer believe in anything. Everything we hope to accomplish is merely a dream. Everything leads to a closed door. There will never be a future. There's only the present. I'm fed up with the future that never comes. Even when it arrives, it's worse than the present."

He paused for a moment as he struggled to control himself before continuing, "I've discovered that I was deceived

101

by everyone: by my university comrades, who are afraid to talk to me for fear of arousing the police's doubts, and by Salwa, who has consented to marry a perfumed corpse whose pockets are stuffed with cash. She's sold out too. All of them have sold out. I've been silenced. What can I do except keep silent? I've grown tired. I'm exhausted. Now I know that we're all dogs. All people are dogs. They've made me hate everything in the world."

I didn't know why Mun'im had changed and what storm had uprooted him. All I knew was that he was weeping. I told him, "Don't cry, Mun'im. At least two people in the world don't belong to the dog species: me and you."

But he screamed at my face, "No! That's not true. I'm a dog too. A dog like any other."

Ashamed to look me in the eye, Mun'im was howling to protest his despair.

Twelve

All the little saplings in the communal garden had matured and grown into lofty trees in the course of two years. I had matured along with them. But how sad I felt on seeing myself grow old while these deep-rooted trees grew more vigorous. The seasons passed in succession—rains, sunshine, spring, and fall—while we reacted to them by carrying our belongings inside and then in summer returning to the outer courtyard, gazing at the stars scattered across the heavens, listening to love-struck vocalists by night.

I didn't like their songs. I had frequently wondered how they could love folk songs like these, which were inflamed by sorrow. The songs themselves were a flood of tears. They were an open wound dripping blood. I didn't want to feel any sadder, because my sorrow could have sufficed for an entire people. How I longed to ask these weepers, "Don't your throats harbor any songs to make us happier?" There they were—sprawled out in their ancient blankets, propped up on pillows, listening to this distressing desolation: a spirit's weeping. I, on the other hand, was thinking about the suns, days, fields, abayas, and nights mentioned in the lyrics, without successfully touching or reaching them. The spasmodic voices alarmed me—perhaps because they lacked self-confidence. They wanted everything. They wept over everything but didn't have enough courage to die for the sake of anything, either. While they slept and rolled around in their beds from an anxiety they would never discuss openly, I watched over them, smoking until dawn's first breezes. Because I recognized this anguish even in their sporadic laughter, I felt they were more innocent than nature itself. In the winters, my task was rougher. Once they had all succumbed to the jaws of bestial sleep, I would hear their shrill moans like a knife-thrust to the side. There was always a man who suddenly would scream, wake up, and lift his head to stare at the sleepers before he fell asleep once more. I wondered what nightmares were pursuing this nocturnal waker. I didn't know. All I really knew were my nightmares, because they never talked about theirs. They were right, or so I assumed, since a person must always have some secrets of his own. Dreams were shared with everyone, but they kept their nightmares to themselves.

I too had my nightmares, in fact one nightmare that was always repeated: while I walk along the street, with nothing on my mind, a crazed truck suddenly swerves toward me. When I try to elude it, I collide with the outward-spiraling spear-tip of a fence. This plunges into my heart, causing blood to flow like an inexhaustible fountain. Then a gray cat approaches and laps up the blood spread over the sidewalk. But he's not satisfied with that. He climbs on me—the bleeding, wounded man impaled on the spear-point—and licks the blood from my heart. From my cross, I watch him, because I recognize him. He's one of the people closest to me.

I ask myself: Why have I been destined to witness my own death, one I can't resist? I occasionally allow the truck to roll over my body when I become exhausted by the spear embedded in my heart and the cats that lick my blood. If I had had enough money, I would have bought a trained dog to protect me. Even so, I didn't hate that cat with the human face. After he became a friend, I searched for him on cold nights.

In each of the four seasons, twice a month, I sat opposite a bit of mirror that I had found soon after entering the penitentiary, in order to shave, merely to continue my acquaintance with my face. I observed my face, which had lost its youthful vigor. I no longer had a full face with a healthy glow. There were wrinkles and black splotches beneath my eyes and on either side of my mouth. My nose remained unchanged and even seemed to have increased in size in this new environment. My face no longer frightened me much, because to some extent I had grown used to it and loved it just for this reason. What frightened me was the tremor of my hands. They were small, and suddenly many veins were visible—blue veins that rose to the surface, pushing up the skin, tempting veins filled with blood. How I would have wished to take a razor to them and scrape them down, but I was afraid my gray cat would see me and come lick the blood. Oh how I wished I could stop these successive seasons, to prevent them from coming. Was it possible for me, who kept close watch on my face, to withstand the minutes, hours, months, days, and years? Oh! It's time that destroys a man, who grows in wisdom as he nears his grave. At the moment of death—what a farce—we are wiser than at any other moment in our life, while everyone else is praying silently.

◼

About a month ago when the last member of the committee was leaving, he took me aside and told me point-blank, "We've decided to transfer leadership in the penitentiary to you. I hope you won't refuse. There's no one else left we can trust besides you."

I hesitated a little before saying, "Fine. I'll try. I believe I've learned a lot from you."

The smiling man answered, "We consider you're one of us, even if you think of yourself as an outsider. We've also learned a lot from you."

When this man passed through the penitentiary's gate, I felt a profound desire to weep. For here I was—a man who had set out to look for a whore in a café. By a ridiculous coincidence, I had become the yard boss of a detention facility for political prisoners. Every day I greeted the new arrivals, encouraging them to believe in themselves, telling them about the new world that would be born from their suffering. None of them asked whether I actually was a leader or merely a passerby drafted to head the ranks. The warden or police supervisor occasionally summoned me for this or that matter related to regulating life in the cell block. The police supervisor told me jovially when I informed him that I had assumed responsibility for the other inmates in their relations with the administration, "My God! What a fool I was when I almost convinced myself that you were here without ever having committed any offense. Do you remember? You told me that you were arrested by mistake while sitting in a café. But now you're taking charge of the most important detention facility for political prisoners. Thank God I wrote a report about you in which I cast doubt on everything you had told us about yourself. Otherwise, I myself would deserve punishment now."

I replied spontaneously, "It's true I attempted to deceive you, but that was futile. I was forced to come clean about my identity in the end. Yes—I'm one of them."

Laughing, the police supervisor, who was feeling cocky about his minor triumph, replied, "That's more like it. A lot better. We don't like a man who has no identity, because we don't know how to treat him."

⊡

I stood at the gate of Cell Block 5, waiting for the arrival of the newly arrested men after the administration had asked me to prepare places for them to sleep. A mature man entered, carrying his bedding on his back, and headed toward the large prison yard, followed by a worker who said it wasn't his first time and that he had previously spent months in this cell block. I didn't recognize him. Perhaps that had been before I arrived in Cell Block 5, which existed before I was born and which perhaps will continue to operate after I die as well. The worker grumbled, "There's another guy who asked to join us."

This was a young man of about twenty-eight with a sad, anguished face. I greeted him, "Young man, come here. You're one of us now. Where's your bag and your bedding?"

He looked at me in dismay. "I don't have bedding or a bag. I was sitting in a café when they arrested me three days ago."

Then he asked me pleadingly, "Do you know when they'll release me? I'm not guilty. I swear I haven't committed any crime."

I placed my hand on his shoulder affectionately and answered, "Don't think too much. Everything will be okay."

He said sorrowfully, "But I want out. Why would they arrest an innocent person like me?"

I declared, as though affirming an eternal verity, "That's not important. What's important is that you're here with us. Isn't that so?"

He said nothing this time; he was gazing at the sunlight on the wall.

Baghdad, Park al-Sa'dun Region
December 1971